The Donut Shop
By James Curl

J.C Publications

Sacramento, Ca

The Donut Shop

James Curl

(ISBN-13): 978-0-692-48459-3

Cover design by Elderlemon Designs

Manufactured in the United States of America

J.C Publications
Sacramento, California
JCPublication.com

Table of Contents:

Chapter one
Grandpa

His father's voice came loudly down the hallway and found its way into his room. "Cody! Hurry up; it's almost time to go."

Yeah, yeah, chill out, thought the teenage boy as he angrily packed his clothing into a large black suitcase. At just sixteen the boy was tall, standing a couple of inches over six feet. On top of his head was a thick pile of unruly brown hair. His eyes were blue and full of life and sparkled when he smiled, but at the moment he wasn't smiling.

The last thing Cody wanted to do on summer vacation was to spend the next week in the country with his grandfather. His dad thought it would be a good idea. "It will give you a chance to get to know your grandpa. Besides, he needs some help around the house cleaning and catching up on yard work," is what his dad said. It wasn't just the boy that was opposed to the visit; Grandpa Ray didn't like visitors. Although Ray and Cody's dad, Mike, spoke often on the phone, Ray was never overly close to his grandson or the rest of the family, and had only visited a few times in the sixteen-years since Cody had been born. Ray was a fiercely independent man and now, at 77, was more than a little cantankerous.

It had taken Mike several calls to convince his father that he could use some help around the house and that it was important to spend some time with his only grandson. Surprisingly, after half a dozen excuses, Ray finally relented and agreed to the visit.

"You ready?" asked Mike as he walked into Cody's room.

"Yeah," replied Cody as he zipped up his suitcase. The boy's melancholy showed on his face.

"Hey, cheer up; it's not the end of the world."

"It is for me," mumbled Cody, looking at his father. "Do I really have to go?" he asked, pleadingly. "All of my friends are hanging out at the river today, and Tommy just got his license, I'm supposed to be getting mine too, you know."

"Yes, I know, and you will as soon as you get back from your grandfather's, I promise. And your buddies will still be here a week from now. Look, we have been over this a hundred times. It's important that you get to know your grandpa. I know you don't get it, but someday you will and I promise you, when you're older, you'll thank me. Let's go."

The ride was only three hours, but to Cody it was an eternity. All he could think about as they sped down the highway was how much fun he was going to miss at the river with his friends. His thoughts then drifted to Molly Thompson, the girl that he liked. Cody sat next to her in class and had even been to her house a few times helping her to pass Algebra. The first time she had invited him over, he was so nervous he couldn't even speak. But when he helped her with math he was relaxed because he knew a lot more about Algebra than her. After a few visits they became friends and Cody was head over heels. Molly was one of the prettiest girls in school and spending time at the river with her seemed like a lot more fun than visiting his grandpa. Sitting in gloomy silence Cody dismissed his thoughts and held tight to his anger making no attempt to talk to his dad. Instead he opened his backpack and pulled out the sword and sorcery book about Viking's he was reading; flipping through the pages he continued where he had left off.

Mike, knowing his son was unhappy, left him alone. He knew what he was doing was right. Mike's thoughts drifted back to a conversation he'd had with Cody's mom Carol last week. Carol wasn't entirely sure it was a good idea to send their son to Grandpa's. "You know how your father is, Mike. He doesn't like company and he's grumpy and kind of scary. And ever since your mother died he's been worse." Mike's mom, June, had passed away of cancer five years ago and Ray had taken it harder than he let on. But, like always, the old man kept his feelings bottled up.

"I know," said Mike, "but Cody needs to know his grandfather. Besides, I think it will do both of them some good to spend time together."

"I guess," said Carol, unconvinced. "But you're going to be the one to tell him and deal with the argument."

Looking up from his book, Cody realized that they were almost to his grandfather's house. Although it had been two years since his last visit he recognized the gas station at the exit they took that led to grandpa's small town. He also noticed that the landscape had changed drastically. No more was he in the big city with its tall buildings, congested traffic and masses of bustling people. This was the country. Trees and tall brown grass lined the sides of the narrow two lane blacktop road. Behind old barbed wire fences cows grazed leisurely and old-style farmhouses and barns dotted the great wide open land. "We're almost there," said Mike with a smile.

Cody gave his dad a quick, angry look and did his best to ignore him.

"Hey, cheer up; you had a lot of fun last time we were here, remember? You drove Grandpa's tractor and went fishing."

Unresponsive, Cody sat in silence.

Pulling into the driveway, Cody recognized his grandfather's white pickup truck, complete with a gun rack and fishing poles sticking out of the bed. "Don't forget your suitcase," said his dad as he put his truck into park.

Cody reached back, grabbed his suitcase and backpack from the extended cab and got out. He followed his dad up to the front door. Mike knocked a few times and a second later a deep, gruff voice said, "Who is it?"

"It's Mike and Cody."

A moment later the door opened wide and the two walked in. Without so much as a hug, Grandpa went back to his lounge chair where he had been watching an old Clint Eastwood Western. "How was the drive?" he asked.

"Fine," answered Mike, taking a seat on the couch. "Cody, you can put your stuff in my old room, that's where you'll be sleeping."

"Ok," mumbled Cody as he headed towards his dad's old room. Cody knew that his dad and Uncle Bill had grown up in the house and that his grandparents had lived here forever.

His dad's old room was medium sized and plainly furnished with a queen sized bed, night stand and a small dark wooden dresser. A silver, old style windup alarm clock with bells sat atop the night stand. Cody threw his backpack and suitcase onto the bed and slid the closet door open; it was empty except for a few hangers.

Walking back down the hallway Cody noticed that across the hall the door to the other bedroom was opened slightly. He knew that the room once belonged to his Uncle Billy years ago. Peeking in the boy saw that the room was now used for storage. There were dozens of boxes and plastic containers stacked halfway to the ceiling and an old wooden shelf with figurines and candles on it. Across the room and completely out of place and time, sat a very old wooden chest reinforced with rusty iron bands that were kept in place with broad headed rivets. The box, at one time had been painted green, but most of its paint had long ago flaked away. Across the front, in faded black letters, the words U.S. ARMY could still be seen. Like some fantastic treasure chest out of a pirate's fairytale it sat and Cody wondered what secrets were hidden within.

Back in the living room Cody took a seat on the couch, next to his dad. While his father and grandfather talked, the boy looked around the front room. There were several old photos of his grandparents on the walls as well as high school graduation pictures of his dad and Uncle Billy. Next to the graduation photo was a picture of Ray being sworn in as

Sheriff. Cody knew that his grandfather had been a police officer for over thirty years.

Cody then turned his attention to his grandfather. Ray was a big man, perhaps 6' 2" and even at 77 years old still looked imposing and strong. He had an impressive full head of thick, gray hair. Under his nose in the style of the Old West was a handlebar mustache that swept out to either side and was twisted to upward curving points at the ends. His most striking feature however was his deep blue eyes. Eyes that Cody could see carried a hint of sadness in them. The boy then noticed the faded green, diamond shaped tattoo on his grandfather's right arm. He had seen it before but had never really paid much attention to it. In the center of the diamond, through a mass of curly gray hair Cody read the words: 5th RANGER BATTALION. For a moment he wondered about the significance of that tattoo and then his thoughts were broken.

"What do you say, are you hungry?" asked his dad.

"Yeah," said Cody; they hadn't eaten since before they had left.

All three piled into Grandpa's truck and drove over to Ray's favorite restaurant, a diner called "Rosie's Country Kitchen." During the drive they passed the "Lancers" high school. "Hey, there's my old high school," said Mike pointing. A few blocks later they arrived at a diner that looked as if it had been there since the 1950s. "Can't believe this place is still here," said Mike as they entered the building, "and it looks exactly the same as it did when I was a kid."

Once inside, a middle-aged lady carrying a handful of menus greeted them. "Hi, Ray, how are you?" she asked with a smile.

"Oh, not too bad, Susan," he answered.

"Would you like a booth today or your regular spot?"

"A booth will be fine."

Walking through the restaurant, several people waved or said hi, Sheriff as Ray passed. Sliding into the booth, Susan handed each of them a menu. "I'll be right back with some water."

"Thanks," said Mike. Then he turned his attention to his father. "So, Dad," he said as he looked through his menu, "what do you have planned for Cody?"

"He can help me clean out the garage and make some dump runs and do some yard work. Maybe even let him drive the tractor, also got a wood pile that I want to move."

"That sounds good," responded Mike, "just what the kid needs is some hard work. Isn't that right, son?"

"I guess," answered Cody looking through his menu.

"Are you ready to order? asked Susan, as she set down a glass of water for each of them.

"Sure," answered Ray. "I'll have the chicken fried steak and some ice tea."

"That sounds good," said Mike. "I'll have the same thing."

"And for you, young man?"

"Chicken fried steak for me too, and a large Sprite," responded Cody.

"Ok," said Susan gathering up the menus. "It will be just a few minutes and I'll be right back with your drinks."

"You know," said Mike "the last time we were here was right before Mom died."

"Yeah, I remember," said Ray, staring out of the large glass window with a vacant, faraway look in his eyes. "This was her favorite restaurant."

Again, Cody caught a hint of sadness in his grandfather's eyes. Mike thought for a moment to ask his father if he ever considered dating but he knew that his dad was old school and had been completely committed to his wife, even in death, so he let the thought pass. "Cody, why don't you tell your grandfather about some of your school activities? Cody is playing football this year and is captain of the chess club."

"Is that so?" asked Ray, showing some interest. "So what position do you play?"

"Quarterback," answered Cody.

"Really," replied Ray, and again Cody caught the faraway look in his grandfather's eyes as Ray seemed to stare right through him. "That's a tough position," said Ray.

A moment of silence followed and then Suzan appeared with a handful of drinks. Setting them down, she said, "Be right back with your food."

"Ok," replied Ray.

A few minutes later Susan returned with three plates of hot food. Setting a plate before each of them she said, "Is there anything else I can get you guys?" All three answered no as they began to eat.

Arriving home they returned to the living room and visited for a while, then took a walk around the old house. During the walk Mike pointed out various places where he and his brother Billy had played and told stories about some of the trouble he, Billy and their friends had gotten into as kids, like the time they nearly caught the garage on fire while playing with diesel fuel. Ray remembered the incident clearly as he was the one who put the fire out.

Their walk ended in the driveway. "Well, I guess I better get going," said Mike. "Carol is waiting and we have to get ready for our trip." Mike and Carol had booked a flight to Florida for four days and Mike was anxious to get back home and start his vacation.

Cody, still angry, gave his dad a quick, unenthusiastic hug.

"I'll see you next Monday," said his father, "and don't give your grandfather a hard time."

"I won't."

Mike then gave his father a hug, which Ray only half heartedly returned. "Make sure you put that boy to work."

"Oh, I will," replied Ray, "you can count on that."

A moment later, Mike drove off with a wave.

Cody followed his grandfather back into the house. Ray turned on the TV and hit play on the VCR. The Clint

Eastwood Western that Ray had been watching when Cody arrived began to play. And then it hit Cody as he sat there in uncomfortable silence with his grandfather; he hardly knew the man at all. But, he would, not knowing it at the moment, get to know the man unlike anyone before him. And as he would soon discover there was far more to his grandfather than he could have ever imagined.

Chapter Two
The Donut Shop

The alarm clock clanged like a fire alarm. Cody reached over and fumbled with it until he found the lever to turn it off. *Stupid alarm,* he thought. A few seconds later his grandfather appeared at the door wearing a brown flannel jacket and red ball cap with a tractor on the front. "You up?"

"Yeah," said the boy, still bleary eyed and half asleep.

"Good, we're leaving in ten minutes, and you better grab a jacket, its cold out there."

Cody rolled out of bed and slowly got dressed. A quick trip to the bathroom and he was ready to go.

He found his grandpa waiting in the front room watching the morning news and taking a pinch from his can of chew. Without a word Ray got up, flicked the TV off and led the way out to his truck. Even though summer was on its way the morning was cold and slightly overcast. "How'd you sleep?" Ray asked.

"Ok," replied Cody.

"Good," said Ray as he started the truck and put the heater in full blast mode.

After a short drive they pulled into the parking lot of an old shopping center and stopped in front of one of the storefronts. Above the entrance was a red neon sign that said open, and painted across the store's large front window, were the words "Stardust Donuts," in sparkling gold letters.

Walking inside Cody was greeted by the cozy warmth of the place and the delicious aroma of hot coffee and freshly baked donuts. "You're late," said a gravelly voice. Cody looked over and saw two really old guys sitting at a horseshoe shaped booth. The man who had spoken was sipping a large coffee and eating a sprinkle donut. His partner was intently reading a newspaper.

"His fault," said Ray, pointing a thumb at Cody.

The boy smiled and shrugged his shoulders.

"Here," said Ray handing his grandson a ten dollar bill. "Get me a large coffee and a cinnamon roll, and get yourself whatever you want."

"Ok," replied Cody. He stepped over to the display case where an assortment of donuts was lined up.

A grey haired woman greeted him from behind the counter with a pleasant smile. "You must be Cody," she said. "Ray told me you were coming to visit. I'm Doris."

Cody responded with a "Hi."

While he eyed the donuts and tried to decide which one he wanted, Doris pulled a big cinnamon roll off the rack and filled a large cup of coffee. "No need to tell me what your granddad wants, I already know; he's only been coming in here for more than 30-years. Now what can I get for you, young man?"

A few minutes later Cody slid into the booth with two cinnamon rolls, a large coffee and a hot chocolate. "So this is your grandson," said the man who had spoken earlier.

"That's right, answered Ray."

"Your grandfather told us you were coming," the man said, smiling and holding out his hand for a shake. "My name is Joe Sullivan."

Cody looked at the man and saw he was heavily wrinkled and only had a few wisps of grey hair covering his bald head. Near the top of his forehead ran a long jagged scar with faint stitching marks. Below the scar he had kind blue eyes and a contagious smile; Cody liked him right away.

Shaking Joe's hand Cody noticed that two of his knuckles were enlarged and lumpy as if they had been broken and never healed properly. He then realized that Joe had a faded tattoo the same as his grandfather's, except that he also had a pair of boxing gloves below it and the words, "Army Middleweight Champion." It was then that Joe's partner lowered his paper and looked over the rim of his glasses. The man had a neatly trimmed mustache and a precise salt and pepper flat-top haircut. "Nice to meet you, young man" he said, as he held out his hand. "My name is Charles, but you can call me Chuck."

"Ok Chuck," said Cody. And he noticed, as he gave Chuck's hand a shake, that he too had the same tattoo as his grandfather and Joe.

A second later there was a commotion at the front door. "God damn it!" came a loud voice. Cody looked over to see a short, broad shouldered, thick-limbed old man on crutches. He was wearing a cowboy hat, a red flannel jacket and the thickest glasses Cody had ever seen. His left leg from the knee down was missing and he was struggling to try and open the door while maintaining a grip on his crutches.

"Do you need me to come over there and hold the door for you, George?" asked Doris.

"Hell no!" growled the old man. Finally, after a few more curse words he made it in and hobbled up to the table, stopping right in front of Cody.

"You're late," said Joe.

"I'm always late. In case you've gone senile from old age let me remind you, I only have one leg. This you're grandson?" asked the man on crutches. His question was directed at Ray, but he was looking at Cody over the rim of his Coke bottle glasses, with a critical eye.

"Yep, that's my grandson," answered Ray, before taking a sip of his coffee.

"Well are you gonna introduce me?"

"Cody, this is George Wilson, George this is Cody."

"Well, Cody," said George as he held out his hand for a shake, "you're in my spot."

Cody shook the broad hand and it was like shaking a piece of iron. The boy then noticed that George's pinky finger was missing and the knuckle was scarred over. As Cody got up George handed him a five dollar bill. "Can you do me a favor, son?" he asked with a smile as he pushed up his glasses that had slid down. "Can you get me a large coffee and two glazed donuts? I've only got one leg," he said with exaggerated sadness as he sat down.

Cody wasn't sure what to make of George, but he did as asked.

Returning to the booth, the young boy handed George his coffee, donuts and change; then grabbed a chair from one of the empty tables and sat down. "So you're from Cincinnati?" asked Joe, "you do any fishing in the big city?"

"No, not really," replied Cody.

"You like fishing?"

"Oh yeah," the boy replied enthusiastically.

"Of course he does," said Ray, "he's a Miller."

"Good, when you get a chance have your granddad bring you over to my place. I have a big pond, filled with catfish and bass."

"Ok," responded Cody, looking at his grandfather.

"Sure, but first we got to make a few dump runs. Maybe after that we can stop by."

With that Ray reached into his pocket and pulled out his chew-can and loaded his bottom lip. "When you gonna give that stuff up?" asked Joe.

"Never!" came Ray's retort. "Hell, I'm 77-years-old, what the hell do I care?"

Joe then laughed and looked at Cody. "You know, your granddad's been chewing that stuff since we were kids. Lucky it hasn't rotted a hole right through his lip. Let me tell you, way back when, before your granddad became sheriff, we drove trucks together for a time. He would spit that stuff out the window while we were driving and by the time we got back home the whole side of the truck would be covered with his sticky chew spit."

"That's gross," said Cody.

"You're telling me," Joe said with a laugh "We had to scrub that stuff off with a brush and a pressure washer."

Just then George asked Cody, "Say, kid, aren't you gonna ask me how I lost my leg?"

"Oh here we go," said Chuck from behind his newspaper. "What's it gonna be this time, shark attack, chainsaw accident?"

"Listen here you old fart, you just sit there and read your newspaper!" snapped George. Chuck just shook his head as he turned the page of his paper. Without waiting for Cody to answer, George turned his attention back to him and said, "Your granddad and I went on a moose hunting trip up in Alaska about 30 years ago. While we were on the trail of a big buck we were suddenly attacked by a giant grizzly, came right out of the bushes with a terrible growl, 10 feet tall and 1,500 pounds. Well, before we shot it dead it bit my leg clean off," and holding up his hand to show Cody, "and my pinky."

Joe laughed, Chuck shook his head. Cody wasn't sure what to think of the story, but he was fairly certain that George was full of it. He looked at his grandfather with a questioning glance and asked in an incredulous tone, "Is that really what happened?"

"That's the way I remember it," answered Ray with a poker-straight face.

Cody sat quietly eating his donut and sipping his hot chocolate. For the next hour his grandfather and the other old men told stories and talked about what they had planned for the week. While he listened Cody got the impression that his grandfather was the leader of the group, and had been for a long time. Occasionally other customers would come in. Some just waved and said "morning," while others would come over and chatted for a while.

Driving back home Cody was thinking about the men at the donut shop. "Grandpa, did George really have his leg and pinky bitten off by a Grizzly bear?" he inquired skeptically.

Ray didn't answer right away. "No," he said finally. "Well how did he lose them?"

"He lost them in World War II." Cody thought about it for a moment. "Were you in World War II? Is that where you got your tattoo?"

After a long pause Ray answered. "Yes, but it's not something I really want to talk about."

Cody could tell by the serious tone of his grandfather's voice that the conversation had hit a brick wall. "Ok," said the boy, letting the subject drop.

It was a about 8:30 when they pulled into the driveway. Ray opened the glove box and pulled out the automatic garage door opener and pressed the button. The door lifted slowly with a squeaking of oil deprived chains. Looking in, Cody saw that that the large, two-car garage was packed from wall to wall with boxes and furniture. "We're gonna load up all of that stuff and take it over to the city dump."

Great, thought the boy, *just how I want to spend my summer vacation.* "Looks like a lot of work."

Ray responded with a, "Yep, it is."

After a quick trip into the house to go to the bathroom Ray loading up a wad of chew and they began. For the next several hours they worked, loading up the truck and driving over to the city dump. Cody, unaccustomed to heavy lifting, tired after a few hours; the only hard work he had ever done was mowing the lawn on Saturday mornings and taking out the trash. His grandfather on the other hand seemed tireless and Cody was amazed at the old man's endurance. Although not fast, Ray just kept marching like a robot back and forth loading the truck. Noticing that his grandson was wearing out after only two dump runs, Ray decided a break for lunch was in order. "Ok boy, let's take a break and get something to eat, sound good?"

"Yeah, I'm starving."

The two sat quietly in the kitchen and ate turkey sandwiches with chips and iced tea. "So," asked Cody. "Do you think we will have time to go fishing at George's today?"

"Probably not," answered Ray. "I figure we can do two more dump runs and then it will be too late for fishing, maybe tomorrow."

"Ok." Cody was a little disappointed but figured he had plenty of time to go fishing, tomorrow.

It was after 6:00 p.m. when they finally arrived home from their last trip to the dump. Cody was worn out and thankful they were through for the day. They had made a big dent in the pile of junk, but Cody knew they would have to make a few more runs before they were finished.

"How about some dinner?" asked his grandfather as they walked into the house.

"That sounds great," replied Cody.

"You like chicken pot pies?"

"Yeah, I love'em."

"Good," said Ray as he pulled four pot pies from the freezer and took them out of their boxes. "Go ahead and get a shower while I get the pies cooking, it will be a while before their done."

"Alright," replied Cody. Heading to his room the boy noticed that the door to his Uncle Bill's room was open. Instantly his attention was drawn to the old chest, and for a time he stared at it wondering again what was inside. He thought for a second about asking his grandfather, but quickly dismissed the idea. *He would probably just get mad,* he thought as he reached over and pulled the door closed.

Back in the kitchen after his shower, Cody found his grandfather setting the kitchen table. "Pies will be done in about 15 minutes," said Ray.

"Great, I'm starving," replied the boy."

"You ever watch any John Wayne movies?" asked Ray.

"No," was Cody's answer.

"Well, you're in for a treat. I got one of his best, called *True Grit*. I'll put it on after dinner."

"Ok," said the boy, sitting down at the table.

With dinner out of the way Cody settled on the couch as Ray rewound the movie and hit play on the VCR. For the next hour and a half they sat and watched. When the movie ended Ray asked, "Well, how'd you like it?"

"It was pretty good, but not enough action," said Cody.

"Not enough action," Ray said incredulously. "You kids and your special effects and action movies," he grumbled while shaking his head. "I think that maybe, you don't know what a good movie is." Ray then got up and pushed the stop button on the VCR. "Anyway, I guess its bedtime," he added as he turned and headed towards his room. "I'll see you in the morning; don't forget to set your alarm."

"Yeah, I think you're right," said Cody, yawning and stretching. "See you in the morning, Grandpa."

Climbing into bed with a yawn, Cody thought about his day. He knew that tomorrow would be another day of hard work and hopefully some fishing. He then thought about the old guys at the donut shop. He was surprised that he had enjoyed them so much and looked forward to seeing them again. Reaching over he flicked the lever on the alarm clock; it would be going off at 6:30 a.m.

Cody sat up in bed and rubbed his eyes. Looking at the clock he saw that it was almost eight and realized that the alarm hadn't gone off. Checking the lever he found that it was in the off position. *I know I set it,* he thought to himself. Yawning, he got up and made his way into the front room. The house was quiet and a little chilly. Pushing the curtains aside he looked out the window and noticed that his grandfather's truck was gone. *Must have gone to the donut shop,* he thought.

Turning around he headed back to his room, but stopped when he noticed that the door to his Uncle Billy's room was wide open. He then thought, *that's weird, I shut that door last night. Grandpa must have opened it.* Immediately his eyes darted to the old Army chest. For a moment he was reluctant and hesitated to enter the room, but an inexplicable urging arose in him, an overwhelming need to find out what mysteries were kept hidden within the old box.

With a squeaking of rusty hinges Cody raised the lid and looked inside. The musty smell of aged wood and paper filled the air around him. Directly on top, was an old green Army jacket with a nametag that read Miller. Judging from its stains and tattered appearance it had seen a lot of action. Pushing the jacket aside the first thing Cody noticed was a handgun lying next to three clips that were filled with bullets. He had seen plenty of guns just like it in the video games he played, and knew it was a military Colt .45. He picked up the weapon, feeling its weight, and wondered if anyone had ever been shot by it.

Putting the gun down the boy reached in and picked up a wooden box with smooth rounded edges, about 4″ wide and 5″ long. He noticed that the wood had at one time been highly polished and was of the finest craftsmanship, but over time it had faded and lost some of its luster. Across the front, carved into the wood, were the words Congressional Medal of Honor. Carefully, Cody opened the lid. Inside, resting on a fuzzy blue velvet cushion was a gleaming Medal in the shape of a five pointed star that looked to be made of solid gold. Encircling the star was a green laurel wreath. Directly in the center, surrounded by the words United States of America, was the image of a woman's head. She was wearing a helmet in the style of an ancient knight and had long flowing hair. The metal was attached to a gold bar that was surmounted to an eagle with outstretched wings. Across the bar was written simply the word "VALOR."

Cody knew, without having to be told, that what he held was something special. He had read of the Medal of Honor in his history books and knew it was the highest award that could be bestowed to a soldier. For a second he contemplated, *Did my grandfather win the Medal of Honor*? He then noticed there were words in sliver letters on the inside of the lid that read: This Congressional Medal of Honor is proudly given to Jake W. Cutter for services above and beyond the call of duty. *Who is Jake*? he wondered.

Cody's attention was then drawn back to the golden Medal. As he stared at it studying its detail he became mesmerized. Unconsciously his eyes closed and he became aware of a presence and felt that he wasn't alone. With a rush a tidal wave of emotions flooded into his body: sorrow, grief, and sadness. The pain was staggering like a physical blow; the boy had never felt such overwhelming heartache before. An instant later, as quickly as it had come the presence was gone and the feelings slowly faded away.

Cody opened his eyes with a jolt and caught his breath. For a few seconds his body tingled with electricity and the hair on the back of his neck was standing straight up, but he didn't have time to ponder the strangeness of it all. It was just then that he heard the rumble of his grandfather's truck pulling into the driveway. Hurriedly, Cody closed the lid on the award and placed it back into the box. He reached up to close the chest but then noticed a curious book that was bound in brown leather, with the word Journal written across the front. Like everything in the box it was old. Its cover was dried and cracked and the paper underneath had turned yellow with the passage of time. For a second he hesitated. It wasn't his and he shouldn't be snooping around, yet something drew him to it, an impulse that he could not deny or explain. Cody snatched up the book, closed the lid and ran into his room. He stuffed the journal under his pillow and returned to the front room.

His grandfather was just coming in the door. "Hi," said Cody, doing his best to act normal.

Ray gave him a quick nod, turned the television on and sat in his recliner.

"How come you didn't wake me up to go to the donut shop?"

"Well, I thought after all the hard work you did yesterday that you might like to sleep in."

"Yeah, I was tired, but I really wanted a donut and some hot chocolate."

"Well good, because I have just that waiting for you in the truck. Go get dressed and let's get to work. If we get enough done maybe we can get over to George's place for a little fishing."

Sometime later they were hard at work piling junk into the bed of the truck. While he worked all Cody could think about was the journal and the strange experience he had. He gave a moment of thought to telling his grandfather what had happened but was way too scared to bring it up. For a while he watched his grandfather load the truck and wondered what he had done in the war. His thoughts then shifted to the journal and what tales it waited to tell.

Turning his attention back to work Cody began moving some large cardboard boxes filled with clothing. It was just then that he discovered a white Schwinn ten-speed bicycle leaning against the garage wall. The rubber on both tires was as cracked as a desert floor and the air had long since leaked out, but the bike still looked to be in decent condition.

"Grandpa."

"Yea?" said Ray.

"Whose ten-speed is this?"

"It was your dad's," said Ray, as he came walking up. "He used to ride that thing everywhere."

Cody brushed the dust from the seat and climbed on.

"You know," said Ray, "I think I have some new tires and inner tubes around here somewhere. A while back I was going to put new tires on it and sell it to a fellow that I know, but he decided not to buy it."

After digging through a cabinet for a while Ray exclaimed, "Here they are." He handed two boxes containing inner tubes to Cody along with two new tires. "There's some tools over in my tool box and a tire pump hiding around here somewhere; and you may want to oil the chain."

Thirty minutes later Cody had the new tires on and was riding up and down the street. Pulling back into the driveway he said, "It works fine."

"Good," said Ray, "then we won't take it to the dump. You can load it in your dad's car and take it home with you."

"I will," said the boy."

"Ok then, let's get this junk to the dump."

They wrapped up work around 4:00 "What do you say we head over to Joe's for some fishing?" asked Ray.

"Sure," answered Cody as he finished stacking some more logs on top of the wood pile; he was beat and some relaxing fishing sounded great.

"All right let's get washed up," said Ray, heading into the house.

Joe's house was only a few miles down the road, but it was farther out in the country. Pulling into the long, gravel driveway Cody could see a white house with a large front porch surrounded by trees. Coming to a stop near the porch they were greeted by three dogs. Two were longhaired, medium sized and mostly brown; the third was a large German Sheppard. Noticing that his grandson looked a little apprehensive Ray said, "Don't worry about the dogs, they won't bite."

Getting out of the truck the boy was nearly knocked over as the dogs crowded around him wagging their tails and sniffing him excitedly. Cody pet each one and could see Joe sitting on the front porch with a grey-haired, heavyset woman. "I was wondering if you were going to make it over today," said Joe.

With the dogs following along Cody and Ray made their way up the front porch.

"This is my wife Ellen," Joe said to Cody.

"Nice to meet you," said the boy.

"Nice to meet you," replied Ellen, with a smile. "Joe told me all about you. Would you like some iced tea? Ray, how about you?"

Both replied with a yes.

"Ok, I'll be right back, said Ellen as she disappeared into the house.

"So you ready for some fishing?" Joe inquired.

"Yeah," replied Cody.

"Good, I got some poles out in the garage all ready to go, got some big night crawlers too; fish love'em."

Just then Ellen returned with two glasses of iced tea, handing one to Cody and one to Ray. "Now before you go I have some chicken that I fried up for you boys." She quickly disappeared back into the house. A few moments later she reappeared with a heaping plate of chicken, covered in foil. "Here you go," she said handing the chicken to Joe. "Good luck with the fishing."

They followed Joe as he led the way out to his garage and equipped each of them with a pole. He then grabbed one for himself, along with a small grey tackle box and a container of worms. "All set," he said with a jovial smile.

A hundred yards behind Joe's house was a pond as big as a football field and roughly the same shape. As they approached, Cody could see fish occasionally coming to the surface and snatching flying insects that dared get too close. Next to the edge of the pond sat half a dozen chairs and a table covered by a large white umbrella. Cody sat down. "Here you go," said Joe, handing Cody a thick, dirt covered worm. "Just put it on your hook and cast it out." Joe then handed one to Ray. Cody found it a little difficult to hook the worm as it wiggled and tried its best not to be impaled, but eventually he got it secured and sent it far out into the water with a smooth overhand cast. *Finally,* he thought as he sat there eating delicious fried chicken and enjoying the afternoon, *I'm having some fun* and then he wondered what his friends were up to back home.

"So, did you get that crap cleared out of the garage, Ray?" Joe inquired between bites of chicken.

"Most of it," answered Ray as he cast his line out and took a seat.

"Good," said Joe.

"You know," Joe said with a chuckle, "your granddad's been threatening to clean that junk pile for years, bout time he got it done."

"Yeah it was a lot of work," responded Cody, as he took a sip of his iced tea. It was just then that Cody was startled to see his pole jerk up and down rapidly and the bobber disappear below the water.

"Looks like you got a bite," said his grandfather. Again the tip of the pole was pulled down, this time harder. "Set the hook," said Ray, "now!"

Cody gripped the rod tight and gave it a quick yank. Instantly the tip began bouncing up and down like a spring. Excitedly, Cody started to reel in the fish. As he did so, a large bass suddenly burst from the pond shaking its head violently in an attempt to break free of the hook; with a splash it disappeared back in to the water.

"Whoa, that's a big one," said Joe with a grin.

"Easy now," Ray cautioned as he stood up from his chair, "don't pull too hard, you don't want to break the line."

Cody eased up a little and continued to crank the reel.

"It was a good fight he put up," said the boy, lifting the wiggling fish out of the water and admiring it.

"Here," said Joe, handing Cody a rusty pair of pliers from the tackle box. "Take the hook out and toss him back in, unless you want to eat'm."

Cody thought about it for a moment then decided to throw him back in.

As the sun was dipping below the horizon, and the fireflies were just starting to blink green, Cody and his grandfather said good-bye to Joe and Ellen. "You coming to the donut shop in the morning?" asked Joe.

"I'll be there," said Ray as he put the truck in drive, "how about you, kid?

"Oh yeah, I'll be there too."

"Good, you can brag to the fellas about all the fish you caught. Ok then, see you in the morning, and don't be late."

With a wave they drove away.

Back home Ray started looking through his collection of videos and asked, "You up for a movie?"

"No, I'm kinda tired. I think I'll take a shower, do a little reading and go to sleep early." Cody's mind kept wandering back to the old journal and he was anxious to read it.

"Suit yourself," said his grandpa, still looking through the row of old movies.

"We are going to the donut shop in the morning, right?" asked Cody before heading down the hallway.

"Yep, bright and early, so set your alarm."

"Ok, I'll see you in the morning."

Cody closed the door behind him and dove into bed. Eagerly he slid the journal out from under his pillow and unbuttoned the flap. As he did so several black and white photographs fell onto his chest. Picking them up, he arranged them into a neat stack and began looking at each one. The first one was a picture of a massive ship engulfed in flames and smoke. The second was of two young men. One of the men, Cody recognized as his grandpa the other was a towering man, with his left arm draped over his grandfather's shoulder. The two were wearing Army uniforms and holding machineguns. Both were smiling happily. Cody thought it odd since he couldn't remember ever seeing his grandfather smile or looking so happy.

The next picture was of a group of five men. His grandfather and four others who resembled Joe, George and Chuck, the old guys from the donut shop. Standing behind them and nearly engulfing them with his long arms, was the big man. Flipping the picture over Cody read, June 10, 1944, France: Ray Miller, Joe "Dempsey" Sullivan, George "Stubby" Wilson, Charles Thorn, Jake Cutter. Cody flipped the picture back over and looked at Jake. *So that's Jake,* he thought. The next two pictures were of different men with his grandfather. When he was done, Cody set the pictures aside and turned to the first page of the journal.

First Lieutenant Ray Miller sat on his cot reading a letter from his girlfriend June. He looked up when he heard echoing footsteps. A man, nearly a giant in stature, approached. "Here you go, Sir," he said, tossing a book onto Ray's bed. "You said you wanted one of these when we joined the Army, nearly two-years ago, remember?" Sitting down next to Ray the cot squeaked and groaned in protest under the man's great weight. "You said you were going to keep a record of our adventures so we could tell our grandkids someday."

Ray picked up the book and saw that it was a brown leather covered journal with a flap and a shiny brass button that keep it closed. "Thanks," he said, "I'll start tomorrow."

"Oh, and happy birthday," said the big man flashing a crooked smile as he got up and walked away.

Ray thumbed through the blank pages and thought about what he would write.

"Damn!" grunted Ray as he completed his 50th pushup. He stood up breathing hard. Looking over to his right was his best friend Jake, to his left his other three close friends: Joe, Chuck and George. Together, the five of them, all from the same small town in Ohio, had joined the Army just days after the Japanese attacked Pearl Harbor. After nearly two years in, and having lived through numerous hair-raising battles, they were back on American soil at Camp Forest, Tennessee; all five had volunteered to be part of the newly formed 5th Ranger Battalion along with over 500 other soldiers. For the next month they were to go through a rigorous physical training program consisting of: hand-to-hand combat, boxing, wrestling, swimming, jogging, speed marches and log drills. In addition, every one of the Rangers had to learn the mechanical function, and qualify with every machinegun, rifle and pistol used by the Army.

Having finished his pushups before Ray, Jake stood wiping the sweat from his brow with a massive hand. Standing next to Jake, Ray felt small; it was a feeling that he had grown accustomed to, having known Jake since they were nine-years-old. He looked up and smiled at the giant. At 6' 7" and 275-pounds Jake was enormous with broad shoulders and lean hips. Smiling, the big man said, "Football training isn't this hard."

Ray chuckled. "Well, when we get back home you'll be in great shape."

"Yeah, I can't wait to get back on the field."

Before joining the Army, Jake had played professional football with the Cincinnati Bullies, and was the best defensive tackles in the country. But it wasn't just his great size that made him an all-star football player; he was incredibly athletic, explosively fast and as strong as any two men in the platoon. Yet, for all his athletic gifts, he was not the typical dumb jock. Jake was smart and had excelled at academics as well as sports. As if his natural athleticism wasn't enough, he was movie star handsome with a thick head of curly brown hair, vibrant blue/grey eyes and strong, chiseled facial features. Hollywood had come calling more than once to offer the young football star a part in a movie. *Some guys have all the luck*, thought Ray.

Being a pro football player made Jake a celebrity among the men. Most of them had seen his picture in the newspapers and had read about his quarterback crushing skills or had listened to his games on the radio. With his larger than life size and easy going personality, Jake was a hero to many of the fellows and was loved by everyone in his platoon.

Ray glanced at his other friends. There was Joe Sullivan, a red haired, green eyed, freckle faced Irishman with a lean build and a dented nose. Joe was the battalion's best sniper and the Army's amateur middleweight boxing champion. Because of his aggressive two-fisted fighting style Joe had earned the nickname "Dempsey" after the former heavyweight champion Jack Dempsey. Standing next to Joe was Chuck, with his straight pointed nose, neatly trimmed mustache and perfect flattop haircut. Chuck wasn't just a good soldier he was also a combat medic. To Chuck's left was George Wilson. At 5' 6" he was short, but thick and as strong as a bull. Everything about George was hard and just bumping into the guy could cause bruises. He may have been a little grumpy and rough around the edges with his unfiltered talk, but he was a loyal friend and as brave as any soldier that had ever donned a uniform. George was playfully called "Stubby" by his friends. His short man's complex didn't like the nickname, but had learned to accept it.

With the pushups completed the physical fitness instructor, Captain Phil Scott yelled, "All right, men, we have a three mile run and then we're done!" In a single file the 35 men of the platoon followed the captain at an easy pace around the campgrounds. Although Ray was a first lieutenant and made a platoon leader when he volunteered for the Rangers, he was under the command of Captain Scott. The advancement to platoon leader was one that Ray deserved. During his nearly two years in service Ray had proven himself a capable leader both with his men and on the battlefield; it was because of that quality that Ray had advanced quickly through the ranks.

While jogging, Ray thought about the rumors he had picked up: reports that the 5th battalion had been formed and was now training to take part in a massive invasion of France, whispered to happen about nine months from now.

After a month of intense combat training at Camp Forest, the entire 5th battalion was moved to Fort Dixon, New Jersey. By now all of the men in the battalion knew that something big was brewing. For the next month the troops underwent more severe physical training as well as weapons qualification. At times the training was too tough and occasionally a soldier would drop out. This was however, to be expected and allowed the Army to make sure that they had only the finest soldiers, both physically and mentally. On December 20, the Battalion was again moved, this time to Camp Kilmer, New Jersey for more training. It was here that the Rangers received word that they would be departing from New York on the ocean liner *RMS Mauretania* on January 8; destination top secret.

Ten days later they made landfall in Liverpool, England where vigorous combat training resumed for the next two months. After England it was off to Scotland where Colonel Max Schneider joined the men and the Battalion endured harsh commando, cliff, and assault training; the most difficult and tiring training that any soldier ever had to endure. Final training concluded in late April with amphibious training, landing operations and the "formal" Fabius II landing exercises.

With preparations out of the way the 5th battalion awaited their orders for what they had heard was called "Operation Neptune," the largest and most daring amphibious invasion the world had ever known.

D-Day, thought Cody as he lowered the journal. He had learned all about it when his history class spent three weeks covering World War Two. To Cody, it didn't seem real that his grandfather was part of that history, so long ago. *D-Day was just stuff in a history book,* or so he thought.

Completely absorbed in the diary, Cody turned the page.

Climbing into the landing craft, Ray and 34 men of the 5th Ranger Battalion were more than a little scared. They had all heard the reports that the Allied Forces were being cut to pieces on the beaches of Normandy. In response to the reports, their commander Colonel Schneider ordered the entire 5th battalion of 563 soldiers diverted to a new rendezvous point. Instead of landing on Dog Green sector of Omaha Beach, they would be landing farther east on Omaha Beach at Dog White. Their objective however was still the same -- to support the Allied troops and help break through the German defenses.

Ray squatted down on his knees along with Jake, George, Chuck and Joe and pulled out his bag of chewing tobacco. Unrolling the bag he lifted out a pinch and placed it between his cheek and gum. A moment later the diesel engine throttled up with a puff of black smoke and the vessel began to move. During the 15 minute ride there was no conversation among the group. Even "Big" Jake, typically fearless in the face of battle, was quiet. Most of the men stood in somber silence nervously smoking cigarettes, while others knelt down holding crosses or rosaries while they prayed.

The LCVP sped through the choppy water bouncing up and down and slamming into the waves. Each time it came down it drenched the troops with a shower of bone chilling water. As they neared the beaches the driver's voice came loudly over the roar of the engine. "Get ready to clear the ramps, one minute to landing!" Gradually the driver throttled down the motor and the craft came to a stop just off the beaches of Normandy.

Looking over the side of the boat for the first time Ray saw hundreds of barrage balloons dotting the skyline. The blimp shaped balloons were anchored in place by steel cables tethered to the ground and used to defend against low flying aircraft attack. Ray then saw that hundreds of iron Tetrahedrons had been set up along the beach. The massive X shaped objects had been placed there to prevent the Allied forces from unloading directly onto the shore. To the left of his position Ray spotted dozens of landing and transport vessels, some capsized and blown to pieces. To his right over 50 more boats were pulling up getting ready to unload troops and equipment. Directly in front of him a fierce battle raged on the smoke covered shoreline. Thousands of Allied troops were battling stiff German resistance as they attempted to breech the Nazi defensive fortifications known as the Atlantic Wall.

The bow ramp slammed down hard shooting a spray of salt water into the air, and the killing began. Bullets from the German machine guns tore through flesh and men fell screaming as they died. In a panic, soldiers jumped over the sides or pushed their way into the water. With his head down Ray jumped over a dead body and leaped into the frigid ocean. The crashing and pounding of the surf nearly knocked him over, but he caught his balance. Close behind was Jake, followed by Dempsey and the rest of his platoon. A quick glance over his shoulder showed Ray, Jake's smiling face. "Up the beach and at them!" he bellowed, charging ahead. *The reckless son of a bitch,* thought Ray as he plowed through the waist deep water.

Hitting the beach, Ray and his platoon scattered and took cover behind several Tetrahedrons. The relentless onslaught of the German machine guns killed four of his men before they could find cover and kept the rest pinned down. Looking around, Ray saw that Omaha Beach was absolute chaos. The deafening blasts of explosions, the rapid fire of heavy machine guns, and the screams of dying men mingled with the roar of tanks and the barking of commands. Mangled corpses lay everywhere and the stench of burnt flesh and blood, mixed with fire and smoke was overpowering. Medics, overwhelmed with the number of injured and dying, scrambled frantically to help while trying not to get shot.

Realizing that there were only two types of people on the beach, those that were dead and those that were going to die, Ray decided his next move quickly. 75 yards up the shore was a long, 4' high sand-wall that ran parallel to the beach. The wall offered better protection from the German guns and hundreds of troops had already massed behind it. "Listen up!" Ray yelled to his men as a tank thundered by completely engulfed in flames and smoke. "Most of the machine gun fire is coming from that concrete bunker in front of us. When the Germans stop to change out the barrels of their guns we're gonna make a run for that sand-wall." A few of the men nodded in agreement. "On my mark we go!" Knowing that the Germans had to change out the barrels of their machine guns frequently because of overheating, Ray waited for a pause in the shooting. The instant the guns stopped Ray screamed, "Go!" and took off running followed by a dozen men. As he ran Ray knew he only had between 5 and 7 seconds before the Germans resumed firing. Many of the men, too terrified to move, were left behind.

Crouching low, Ray and his men sprinted as bullets whizzed by and the ground trembled violently from heavy artillery explosions. At about the halfway point the Germans started firing again; three of the men following Ray fell, torn to bloody pieces.

Dropping behind the sand-wall, Ray and his group were instantly pinned down by murderous machine gun fire coming from the concrete bunker. Gathering himself, Ray realized that less than a third of his platoon had made it from the landing craft to the sand-wall. With all of the confusion, he wasn't sure if the other members of his team were dead, alive or lost.

Ray's thoughts were suddenly interrupted by a blast like a thunderclap. A mortar shell had discharged near a group of soldiers only a few dozen yards away. The explosion sent a shock wave of blood, limbs and screaming bodies hurtling through the air.

Recovering from the blast, Ray realized that the heavy mortar fire had come from a machine gun nest about 70 yards up the beach, manned by six Germans. As he watched, the enemy soldiers were in the process of aiming the mortar and reloading it for another shot. "Dempsey!" yelled Ray, "take those bastards down." With the unerring efficiency of an expert sniper Dempsey brought his Springfield rifle into firing position and made a quick adjustment to the scope; a split second later one of the Germans was down with a bullet through his head. Recognizing the work of a sniper, the dead man's comrades dove for cover behind a wall of sand bags. "Keep an eye on them!" Ray shouted. Dempsey nodded.

Turning to a group of soldiers from the 2nd Rangers Battalion, Ray asked, "Where is your C.O?"

"Dead!" answered a young soldier.

"Well who the hell is in charge here!?" Ray demanded.

"Nobody, sir, we're on our own!"

Ray looked around and spotted several soldiers from his 5th battalion. "Where's Colonel Schneider?" he asked a soldier he knew as Tom.

"He's pinned down on the beach," replied Tom, pointing.

Ray looked down the beach and spotted the colonel and dozens of men from the 5th taking cover behind some of the Tetrahedrons.

"Well, where's our captain?"

"Over there," responded the soldier, pointing to a body that had been blown in half.

With the colonel occupied with staying alive and the captain dead, that left Platoon leader and First Lieutenant Ray in charge. For Ray, to think was to act. In an instant his natural leadership abilities took over. Turning to his men Ray yelled, "You guys listen up. Jake, Jimmy and Chuck you're coming with me. We're going to charge that nest and hit them with some grenades while Dempsey and Stubby cover us. It's our only chance. If they get off one more mortar round we're all dead." Ray unstrung his Thompson machine gun and handed it to Dempsey along with two extra 20 round clips. "There's a spot over there," said Ray, pointing as a spray of deadly machine gun fire kicked up a shower of sand just a few feet away. "That's been cleared away by Bangalore's." Ray then turned to the remaining members of his group. "The rest of you men help those guys from the 2nd getting some more Bangalore's up here. We need to blow some more holes through the barbed wire. Then get up there and take out that goddamned bunker."

Following Ray's lead, Jake, Jimmy, and Chuck took off running. The Germans, peeking over their sandbags spotted them and sent a burst of hell fire from their MG42's. Dempsey and Stubby took aim and unleashed a hail of lead from their machine guns that stopped any further thoughts the Germans had about continuing their assault.

Hitting the ground, Ray and his men readied themselves as Dempsey and Stubby reloaded. Each man pulled out a grenade and awaited Ray's signal. From their position it was about a 70 yard dash up a hill and through a living nightmare of bullets, smoke and explosions. Ray knew that there was little chance of making it to the nest alive. Looking at his men, he shouted over the roar of machine guns and artillery fire, "You ready?"

His eyes caught Jake's. The giant gave his familiar crooked smile and said, "As ready as I'll ever be." Ray leaped up and signaled Dempsey as he tore off up the hill. Dempsey and Stubby immediately fired sustained bursts at the Germans keeping them pinned down under a blitz of bullets.

With adrenaline pumping, Ray and his team ran over the rugged, irregular terrain; leaping over low spots and dodging razor sharp barbed wire. The dirt, soft and deep, slowed them down considerably and in no time their breathing became labored. Halfway up the hill an explosion boomed and the ground rocked as if shaken by an earthquake, sending Ray and his men sprawling. The volcanic force of the blast sent red hot shrapnel sizzling through the air. Like a razor of fire a jagged piece cut across Ray's shoulder. "Son of a bitch!" he exclaimed, as his dazed brain recoiled in agony.

Back on their feet the group continued their suicidal dash up the hill. Through thick, black smoke that watered their eyes and burned their lungs they came within throwing distance. Ray could hear the sounds of Dempsey's and Stubby's machine guns and could see that they were keeping the Germans pinned. Thirty feet from the target Ray pulled the safety pin from his grenade. Just as he readied his throw Dempsey and Stubby stopped firing to reload. In that instant one of the Germans rose up. Spotting Ray and his men he opened fire with his rifle. Two bullets struck Jimmy full in the chest blowing out a large portion of his back and innards. He fell screaming as Chuck dropped down to help. Reloaded, Dempsey and Stubby resumed firing, blasting the German in the process. At that moment, Ray threw his grenade followed by Jake's. A second later two thunderous explosions ripped through the machine gun nest. Pulling his .45 Ray and Jake approached cautiously.

Without warning a bloody German soldier stood up. Hit by the grenade explosions the soldier's face and body were horribly wounded. Burnt, blood covered flesh hung down in ragged strips from the left side of his jaw exposing his shattered teeth. With a terrible scream that resonated above the din of battle he raised his submachine gun as Ray and Jake fired simultaneously. Ray's bullet blasted a hole through his enemy's throat, while three bullets from Jake's grease gun took the man through the chest. With a gurgling sound the German tumbled over the wall of sandbags and slid down the hill, his lifeless body coming to rest at Ray's feet.

Looking into the gun pit Ray and Jake found what they expected; five dead Germans. A moment later Chuck came running up, "Jimmy is dead," he panted. Without a word Ray signaled to Dempsey and Stubby as the three huddled behind the sandbags for cover.

All over the beach the battle continued to rage, but for a moment Ray and his men had a respite. With Dempsey and Stubby back in the group Ray decided on their next move. But first Chuck took a look at Ray's injured shoulder. "You're all right for now, sir," said Chuck, after applying some antiseptic and a bandage, "but you're going to need to get it stitched up later." "Let's go," said Ray moving his shoulder to relieve some of the stiffness that was already setting in.

Ray could see that the men of the 2nd had broken through the barbed wire and were waging a full-scale assault on the concrete pillbox. They were halfway up the hill but the Germans were holding strong. "We're gonna get behind that bunker and attack them from the rear."

A short climb and the men crested the hill, but hastily dropped onto their bellies. Two German soldiers, unaware of Ray and his men ran down a long trench towards the bunker. Once they were past Ray signaled his men to follow. They jumped down into the 5' deep trench with Dempsey and Chuck guarding the rear. A short run brought them to the spot where the ditch opened wide at the rear of the bunker and into a patio area. The trench walls, built up higher here, continued around to encircle the fortress. Stopping, the group instinctively squatted down with Dempsey and Chuck guarding the rear about 20 feet back. Ray could hear the firing of the MG42's and knew that the deadly gun, known as "Hitler's Buzzsaw" was raining death on the Allied forces.

"Jake, give me a grenade." "It's my last one," said Jake as he unclipped it and handed it to Ray. Taking the grenade, Ray strung his Thompson over his shoulder, unclipped his last grenade and said, "Wait here." Jake nodded, raising his grease gun to cover his friend. Pulling both pins, Ray ran over to the opening in a crouch and tossed in both grenades. He turned and ran back just in time to take cover as the grenades exploded, sending out smoke and debris. A moment later two tattered and bloody Germans emerged. Seeing his enemy, Jake pulled the trigger of his grease gun cutting both men down.

Suddenly there was a warning from Dempsey. "We've got company!" Dempsey could see a hundred feet straight down the trench and had spotted German soldiers. A second later the lead German began firing. "Move it!" shouted Ray as bullets impacted the trench walls. They hustled out of the trench into the patio area and took cover behind either side of the opening; Ray and Jake to the left, Stubby, Chuck and Dempsey to the right. Ray looked into the trench and returned fire, forcing the Germans to retreat a little and take cover behind a curve in the trench wall. "How many did you see, Dempsey?" asked Ray.

"At least ten, sir."

Outgunned, Ray knew they couldn't hold the Germans off for long and it would only be a matter of time before their enemies climbed out of the trench and surrounded them. Looking around for an escape route, Ray was forced to take cover as a spray of machine gun bullets splattered into the trench wall next to him. Ray's next move was decided out of necessity. "Everyone into the bunker!" he ordered. Ray didn't like the idea of retreating into the concrete building, but had little choice. If they went back down the beach they took a chance of being mistaken for Germans and killed by friendly fire. Running into the bunker, they were trapped, but at least they had shelter and a defendable position.

Darting into the building they were followed by a hail of German bullets that blew chunks out of the concrete walls. Ray, the last to go, sent a quick spray of return fire and then ran in. The inside of the bunker was a mess. The grenades Ray had thrown in had blown guns and ammo everywhere, along with four dead Germans. Suddenly a German stick grenade known as a "Potato Masher" came through the entrance hitting the ground and rolling towards Jake. "Shit!" Stubby shrieked as he dove for cover. The others all hit the deck, too, flattening themselves on the floor and bracing for the explosion. With agility that belied his size, Jake sprang, grabbed the grenade and tossed it back outside. An instant later the report of an explosion sent smoke and soot into their fort.

"Ray, we gotta get the hell out of here!" Dempsey exclaimed as he stood back up brushing himself off.

"Yeah, I know," snarled Ray.

Not waiting around for orders, Jake slung his grease gun over his shoulder and picked up one of the German MG42 machine guns. The Mouser, a massive weapon twice as big and three times as heavy as a normal machine gun was never meant to be used as a hand held weapon, but in Jake's huge hands it fit. The big man looked at Ray as he hefted the gun and smiled. "They'll never expect this." Ray eyed the grim weapon for a second and said, "Ok, we blast our way out. Over the wall and back down the cliff and hope they don't mistake us for Germans."

Looking out of the entrance Ray could see the opening of the trench, but only a few feet in. He spotted no Germans, but knew that like a predator they were laying in wait. "Go!" Ray was out first followed by Jake and Stubby. In an instant a German command was yelled. Six Germans hiding atop the trench sprang up while three burst forth from the opening. A quick but fierce gun battle ensued. Ray and Stubby fired on the three that had come out of the trench opening. Two fell immediately. The third got off several rounds from his submachine gun before being hit by half a dozen rounds. One of the German's bullets struck Stubby in his right hand tearing off his pinky and shattering the handle of his gun. With a cry of pain Stubby dropped to the ground clutching his bloodied hand. Jake, seeing the Germans rise atop the trench, raised the heavy machine gun as if it weighed nothing. In a normal man's hands the gun would have been too powerful and unwieldy to fire, but with his giant like strength Jake held the gun steady and squeezed the trigger. With an ear splitting discharge of bullets, the big man cut a swath of bloody destruction. He saw the fear flash before the Germans' eyes as they instantly recognized the death they faced, but they were mowed down before they could react. And as abruptly as it had begun it was over.

Seeing his friend was down, Ray quickly stepped over and crouched next to him. "George! are you all right?"

"The bastard shot my pinky off!"

"How bad is it? Let me see."

"It's not that bad, sir," Stubby insisted, holding up his bloodied hand. Seeing that his friend wasn't mortally wounded, Ray breathed a sigh of relief.

Chuck, who was next to Ray was already unloading his med kit. "Bandage him up and let's get the hell out of here," Ray ordered.

"I'm on it, sir," came Chuck's reply.

At that moment Dempsey, having climbed atop the trench to get a look around shouted down to Ray, "Better hurry up, there's more Germans coming down the trench."

A second later the group was surprised to see a large group of soldiers climbing up the hill. Ray and his men were quick to bring up their guns but lowered them just as fast when they realized the soldiers were American.

With no time for pleasantries Ray said, "There's a detachment of Germans coming down the trench." One of the men barked an order. "You men get up there and secure that trench." Without hesitation the soldiers double timed it to the top of the hill. The man who gave the order approached Ray, but his attention was drawn to Jake. His eyes widened in surprise and unbelief as he noticed the tall, powerfully built man holding the German gun. Standing like some super soldier, Jake gave the man a smile. "I'm glad you're on our side," said the man as he turned his attention back to Ray. "Name's Kovak, Captain Len Kovak 2nd Battalion, you in charge here?" "Yes, sir," answered Ray, as they saluted and shook hands. "That was until you got here, Captain."

Just then the chatter of rapid machine gun fire coming from the direction of the trench reached their ears. Instinctively everyone took cover next to the trench walls. As they stood listening to the gunfight Len said to Ray, "The Allied forces have broken through some of the German defenses and secured large portions of the beach. There's a camp being set up with a medic station not far from here, looks to me like you need to get your man there."

Just then a soldier came running up. "Captain, we've captured a bunch of Germans." "Good work, Mike. Secure the trench and hold the position." "Yes, sir," replied the private as he turned and ran off. Len then returned his attention to Ray. "Come with me. I'll get you guys over to the camp." "Sounds good, sir," replied Ray. Looking over at Stubby, Ray could see that Chuck had finished and was in the process of re-packing his medic supplies.

"You guys ready?"

"Lead the way, sir," answered Chuck.

Back on the beach Ray found that Dog White was secure and the fighting had subsided. However, distant machine gun fire and sporadic explosions could still be heard further up the beach. From his vantage point on the hill Ray could see that the beach was buzzing with activity. Hundreds of landing craft were scattered along the shoreline unloading thousands of troops and equipment. German captives with hands behind their heads were being led to makeshift prisons, men in jeeps sped by and medics worked frantically on the wounded. It was then that Ray realized the appalling number of dead strewn about the beach and for a moment an emotional blow like a punch to his gut threatened to overtake him. There were hundreds of fallen soldiers as far as the eye could see; the price in blood that the Allied forces had paid to win the beach had been steep. So shocking and unbelievable was the sight, that Ray would carry the image with him until his last day. And he knew, as his mind absorbed the horrific scene that he could count himself among the lucky ones to have stormed the beaches of Normandy and lived to tell about it.

Cody lowered the journal. He was in disbelief that his grandfather and the old men at the donut shop had done what he had just read. *There's no way,* he thought, as he closed the journal and slid it back under his pillow. For a time he laid there thinking about his grandfather; little did he suspect, as he turned off the lights and drifted into slumber, that what he had just read was only the beginning.

Cody awoke with a jolt, his heart racing; he had been dreaming that he was fighting on the beaches of Normandy alongside his grandfather. For a moment he laid unmoving while his pulse slowed and reality came flooding back to him. Glancing over at the clock he realized it wasn't going to go off for another thirty minutes. Without waiting he flicked off the lever, got out of bed and put his clothes on. He was anxious to get to the donut shop and see the men he had read about and he was excited to see his grandfather.

"You're up a little early," said Ray when Cody came walking into the living room. Ray was perusing the local paper and having a chew as the weatherman gave his forecast, which called for scattered showers throughout the day.

"Yeah, couldn't sleep," responded the boy.

"You ready to get a donut?" asked Ray

"I sure am," Cody said.

During the drive the youngster desperately wanted to ask his grandfather about the war, the Journal and the beaches of Normandy, but he was again too nervous to bring the subject up.

Walking inside the donut shop Cody found that the place was packed and customers were lined up at the cash register. He spotted Joe, George and Chuck already seated at their booth sipping coffee and eating donuts.

"Go ahead and grab a seat," said Ray. "I'll get the goods."

Cody pulled up a chair next to the booth and sat down. "Hi," he said.

"Morning," Joe and Chuck greeted him.

"So, Joe here tells me you pulled the biggest fish he's ever seen from his pond," said George with a mouthful of glazed donut. "Kind of hard to believe," he continued with a doubtful tone, "since the biggest fish ever caught from his pond, was by me, last summer."

"Don't listen to him, Cody," said Chuck, from behind his newspaper. "The only thing George ever caught from that pond was a sorry little catfish."

"Listen here, Charles, you just keep quiet." Chuck shook his head with a playful smile and resumed reading his paper. Joe laughed.

"Now, as I was saying," continued George. "I caught a seven pounder. How big was yours, kid?"

Before Cody could answer, his Grandfather cut in. "Bigger than the one you caught, by at least a pound," he said, as he walked up with a tray containing a large coffee, two cinnamon rolls and a hot chocolate. "Here you go," he said, handing Cody his drink and donut. With a look of doubt, George pushed up his glasses up and took a bite of his glazed donut.

"So, what do you guys have planned for the day?" Joe asked.

"Not much," Ray answered. "Looks like it'll be raining off and on all day, probably just watch a couple of movies and take it easy."

"Yeah, can't do much with this rain," agreed Joe, taking a sip of his coffee.

Cody sat silent just watching and listening to the men talk. But now it was with a sense of admiration. And then his mind drifted back to the stories in the journal and the overwhelming emotions he'd felt. He thought about Jake and wanted to ask them if he were still alive and where he was. The urge was nearly irresistible, but he stayed his tongue.

By the time they left the donut shop the rain had started with a light downpour. Pulling into the driveway Ray said, "Run over there and grab a couple of logs off the wood pile, I'm going to make a fire."

"Ok," said Cody.

Removing the tarp covering, Cody grabbed three big logs. Back in the house the boy found his grandfather cleaning the dusty grey ashes out of the fire place. He set the logs down and took a seat on the couch. Watching his grandfather he couldn't help but think about the journal and was anxious to read more.

With practiced hands Ray had a warm, crackling fire going in no time. Taking a seat on his recliner, he opened his newspaper and pulled out a can of chew. "Looks like a good idea," said Cody "I think I'll go lay down and read a little of my book."

"Ok," said Ray scanning through the sports section.

"If the rain lets up maybe we will head over to Rosie's for some lunch."

"Alright," said the boy heading down the hallway.

Cody opened his backpack and pulled out the book he had been reading during the drive to his grandfather's house. He set it within easy reach just in case his grandfather came in unannounced, then reached under the mattress and slid the journal out. In moments he was back in France.

Two days after the liberation of France commenced, Ray and what remained of the 5th battalion were stationed in the city of Foucarville, with the duty of guarding several hundred German prisoners. The city had a large population of about ten thousand people and numerous pubs that got a lot of business from the visiting serviceman. The people of Foucarville, happy to have the Germans rousted, welcomed the liberating troops with open arms. Free of the oppressive German control the town was now in full celebration mode and Ray was able to wrangle a twenty-four-hour pass for himself and a few of his close friends for a little R&R.

"You guys almost ready?" asked Ray.

"Yeah," was the collective answer from the fellas as they combed their hair, brushed their teeth and tucked in their

Army-issue uniforms. It was the first time in months that they had the opportunity for a night on the town.

A short time later the excited group piled into a jeep, moving equipment and ammo to make enough room for everyone. After a bumpy five mile ride they pulled into downtown Foucarville. Ray was told that the most popular pub in town was the Pub Mason, which they found after asking for directions from a group of drunken British soldiers.

Through a narrow doorway that Jake had to duck to enter, the group made their way into the bar. The place was large and illuminated with the faint glow from dozens of smokey oil lamps hooked to the walls. In the middle of the pub was a square, wooden bar surrounded by customers sitting on stools, drinking and smoking. Three bartenders hurriedly took orders and served up drinks.

Ray and the fellas found some empty tables near an exit at the rear of the tavern that led to an outside patio. A moment later an attractive, dark haired waitress appeared. Smiling, she said in English overlaid with a French accent, "Hello, I am Adela." Noticing Jake, her eyes lingered on the big man for a moment.

"You are Americans?" she asked.

"Yes!" came their simultaneous answer. She smiled at their enthusiastic response.

"What I can bring you?"

"Four pitchers of beer," answered Ray, handing her some money.

"I be right back," she said smiling as she turned and headed for the bar.

"I think I'm in love," said George, as they all watched the hypnotic sway of her hips as she walked away.

"George, she's at least four inches taller than you," said Chuck. Ray, Joe and Jake howled with laughter at the comment.

"Hey, that's fine with me," said George. "I don't mind. Oh, and go to hell, Charles."

Although it was early evening the place was already starting to fill up with locals as well as allied soldiers. A few minutes later Adela returned with glasses for everyone and four large pitchers of foam-topped, "stout" French beer. Setting the drinks down she leaned in close to Ray and asked, "The big man, he is somebody, famous, yes?"

"Yes he is," said Ray with a smile, "he's Jake Cutter, a famous football player."

Smiling, Adela then pointing to a group of a dozen soldiers gathered at the main bar and said, "Those men over there, they want to meet with him, yes?"

"Sure," said Ray, "bring them over."

He turned to his friend. "Hey, Jake, it looks like you have some fans here that want to meet you."

"Alright," said Jake with a boyish grin.

With a wave Adela motioned the group over. The excited soldiers swarmed on Jake shaking hands with him, asking for autographs and offering to buy him drinks. One of the men, a photographer with a camera hanging around his neck, suggested pictures. In no time the camera was flashing brightly. Like a flood, word spread quickly throughout the bar about the giant American football player and suddenly everyone was squeezing in to get a shot with big Jake.

Leaving Jake to his adoring fans Ray turned his attention back to the fellas.

"Now remember, Dempsey," Ray said as he filled a class of beer, "you have a match tomorrow." Being the battalion middleweight champion Joe had been challenged by Frank Rizzo, a tough Italian kid from New York. After getting permission from their captain, who thought a friendly boxing match would be good for the boys, Joe agreed to the bout.

"I know, I'll take it easy, sir," replied Joe, rolling his eyes as he took a sip of the thick, dark brew. Ray knew from experience that Joe loved a good drink, and if left unchecked would go all night.

A dozen pitchers and several hours later the pub had filled to overflowing. The noise level had risen to the rafters and the walls shook with the roar of wild, drunken laughter that mixed with music from a jazz band that had sprang up and begun to play. Coming back from the bathroom Ray noticed that a large raucous group had gathered on the outside patio. Curious, he made his way outside to find out what had everyone so animated.

Squeezing his way through the crowd Ray found a bald headed, bull of a man seated at a table. He was arm wrestling a much smaller fellow, who was having no luck putting the big man's arm down. A young soldier, dressed in a British uniform and acting as referee, stood next to the large man, puffing on a cigarette. He spoke to the arm wrestler in a foreign language and raised the big man's hand in victory after he had easily defeated his opponent. Turning to a British soldier who was watching, Ray gathered that the huge man was named Svend Magnason from Norway. Sven was part of a group of Norwegian soldiers under British command that had taken part in the Normandy invasion. He was also the Norwegian arm wrestling champion and claimed to have defeated over 500 men, without a loss. He was now taking on all comers for a bet of just a few Francs.

Ray returned to his table and told the fellows what was going on. He then suggested that Jake give the arm wrestler a go. At first, Jake balked, saying, "I'm not an arm wrestler, I'm a football player."

"Oh, come on, Jake," said Ray, "go show that big bum some real strength and win us some money."

Finally, after the fellows began questioning his manhood, Jake caved in.

"Ok, you guys give me all the money you have," demanded Ray, "we're gonna bet it all on Jake."

"What, are you kidding?" asked Joe. "What if Jake loses? We won't have any money for beer."

"Yeah," said George.

"They have a point, Sir," added Chuck.

"Trust me, fellas, he won't lose," answered Ray confidently.

Looking up at the big man, Jake's crooked smile spread across his face.

"I'll give it my best shot, Sir."

Ray held out his hand. Reluctantly, and not without a share of grumbling from each, everyone handed over what little money they had.

As the latest victim left the table the crowd parted to let Jake and his group through. Everyone stared up in amazement as the towering American approached the table and stood before the arm wrestler. Standing up, as was his custom to greet each new challenger, the big Norwegian loomed before Jake. Not quite as tall but much heavier, the man was dauntingly enormous. Where Jake was leaner at the hips and looked more the athlete, the giant Norwegian was fleshier and more barrel chested. The great sweep of his mighty shoulders was breathtaking and his huge arms bulged with thick, powerful muscles that threatened to rip the seams of his t-shirt. His broad hands and thick fingers were the largest Jake had ever seen.

Motioning towards the referee the man said in English, with a heavy Norwegian accent, "My friend here tells me you are the famous American football player, Jake Cutter. I have heard of you."

"Yep, that's me," was Jake's humble reply.

"Good, then this will be a great victory for me."

With that the crowd went silent and the combatants' eyes locked as they sat. Ray handed over all the money that he had gathered, which amounted to $52.00. Quickly the little referee counted it and shook his head to confirm that they could cover the bet.

Their hands came together, each grasping the other in a vice like grip. Feeling Jake's strength the Norwegian's eyes widened briefly in surprise. The little referee reached over and clasped their hands. Holding them for a moment he then counted, "One, two, three!" And let go.

Instantaneously both men exerted their titanic strength against the other and knots and lumps and masses of iron corded muscles bulged on biceps and forearms. For what seemed an eternity, but was only a matter of seconds, the two were as rigid as iron statues. The only movement was the flexing of powerful muscles and the rising and falling of their mighty chests. Their faces showed the great strain of their efforts as a war of strength and will raged that would have snapped the arms of lesser men. Gradually, the immovability of the two gave way as Jake's strength began to overpower the Norwegian's. Slowly and inexorably he began to force his opponent's arm down, further and further. With a beast like grunt, Svend redoubled his effort throwing in the full weight of his colossal shoulders. Sweat beaded his forehead and the thick blue veins in his arm pulsed and were near bursting with his herculean effort. But Jake's strength was as unstoppable as a juggernaut. At the halfway point of being put down Svend's arm gave out and slammed hard into the beer-stained table with a crash. The crowd erupted in an uproar of yells and clapping as Jake raised his arms in victory. Ray turned to Joe with a huge smile.

"Told you he would win, nobody is stronger than Jake."

But a moment later the hooting and hollering stopped and everyone fell silent.

The big Norwegian, rubbing his aching arm was looking at Jake; his eyes blazing with menace. The little referee stood by nervously puffing his cigarette. Ray, instantly aware of the dangerous situation readied himself for a fight. Instinctively, Joe, George and Chuck were ready to follow Ray's lead.

For a few seconds the situation held like a bomb that was ready to explode as Jake and Svend were locked in a fierce, unfaltering stare down. And then suddenly the tension snapped when the giant Norwegian's scowl turned to a broad, crooked toothed smile. He roared with deep laughter and slapped Jake's shoulder saying, "You a very strong man, the strongest I ever met. Come, let me buy you drink, I am big fan of American football."

Ray let out the breath that he had been subconsciously holding and smiled at Joe.

"That was a little scary," he said. "Naw, the bigger they are the harder they fall," replied Joe.

"Say," said Ray, "that reminds me, you better slow down, remember your fight tomorrow."

"Don't worry about me, Sir; I'm ready for that bum Rizzo." With that Joe took a long swill of his beer, and winked at Ray.

It didn't take long for Jake and Svend to become fast friends, in fact they had a lot in common besides their great size and strength. Much like Jake, Sven was a professional athlete back in Norway. Besides being a champion arm wrestler he was also a professional wrestler and strongman competitor. But, it was the American game of football that really interested Svend. He sat and listened intently as Jake explained the finer points of the game and told stories about other famous football players.

"Ray!" shouted George over the noise of the bar.

"Yeah," responded Ray.

"I'm going across the street and get a tattoo."

Across the street from the pub George had noticed a tattoo parlor/café and smoke shop. A sign hanging out front read: "Le Tatouage Café." Ray knew that George had wanted to get a tattoo and had been talking about doing it for a long while.

"What? You're drunk, Stubby," said Ray. "Go sit down."

"You're damn right I'm drunk, Sir," replied George staggering a little. "But I'm still gonna get a tattoo."

With that George turned and headed toward the exit. Ray sat for a moment and watched him leave. *Ahh hell*, he thought. *I better go after him, keep him from doing something stupid.*

"Joe! Chuck! Jake!" hollered Ray. All three looked over at Ray.

"Let's go, George is headed across the street to get a tattoo."

"What," said Joe, "you serious?"

"Yeah, I'm serious," answered Ray as he pushed his way out of the crowded pub and into the cool night.

Exiting the pub Ray found that the town was alive with activity. With the German enforced curfew no longer in effect, townspeople freely walked the streets and sat outside of smoke shops and cafes. Crossing the street the fellows were careful not to get run over by one of the many jeeps that sped by, overflowing with young soldiers looking for places to drink.

Ray and the guys found George in the "Tatouage" talking to the tattooist and showing him a piece of paper.

"This is what I want. Can you do this right here?" asked George, pointing to his right forearm and shouting a little in his drunkenness.

Some of the patrons, attracted by George's loud voice watched in amusement. The artist, a slight man with a slim build spoke only a little English, but understood clearly what George wanted. "Oui, Oui," he said pointing to a chair and motioning for George to sit.

Snatching the paper from George, Ray said, "Let me see what you got there."

"Hey, give that back!" shouted George, with a hint or anger in his voice.

"Hold up, let me see what it say's."

On a plain white paper George had written the words: U.S. Army, 5th Ranger Battalion, surrounded by the outline of a diamond. Ray read it and handed the paper to Joe who showed it to Jake and Chuck.

"You know that's not bad," said Joe, still holding a glass of beer and taking a sip.

"Tell you what; if you get one, I'll get one too."

"Ray, how about it? You in?" asked Joe.

Ray considered it for a moment, and then looked up at Jake.

"Is it going to hurt?" asked the big man, "you know I'm afraid of needles."

"You big overgrown sissy," said Ray chuckling. He then glanced over at Chuck. Knowing that he was the biggest square in the group, Ray was sure he would refuse.

Maybe it was the alcohol, but to Ray's surprise Chuck agreed without hesitation, saying, "Sure, Joe, you do it and I'll do it."

Ray paused for a moment, in thought. *What the hell, I could be dead tomorrow.*

"All right," said Ray, "who's first?"

An hour later the group stumbled out of the tattoo parlor, each with a new tattoo. Back at the pub Ray and the guys found Svend and his group merrily singing along with the band and well into their drinks.

"Let us have a look," said Svend as Ray and the fellows showed off their new ink.

It was nearing 2:30 a.m. when they started herding everyone out of the pub. Standing out front Ray and his group bid Svend and his friends' good-bye. Over emotional from the alcohol and bonded by their arm wrestling match, Jack and Svend embraced in a fierce, bear like hug that might have cracked the spine of a normal man. The two giants then exchanged addresses and promised to keep in touch after the war.

"I'm driving," announced George with a drunken slur, as they approached the Jeep.

"Like hell you are, Stubby," retorted Joe, in an equally obnoxious, drunken voice. Pushing George aside, Joe made to get into the driver's seat; holding a glass of beer that he managed to slip out of the bar. Despite Ray's suggestion that he "take it easy" Joe had drank without concern.

Before he could get into the driver's seat Ray pulled him away.

"Neither of you are driving, you'll both get us all killed."

"Chuck, you can drive."

"Whatever you say, Sir."

Knowing that Chuck wasn't a big drinker and the least intoxicated of the group, Ray felt that he had the best chance of getting everyone back to the base in one piece. Climbing into the driver's seat, Chuck waited for everyone to get settled. "Hang on," he warned before speeding off.

It was just past 3:00 a.m. when Ray and the boys staggered up to the large tent that served as their barracks

"Now everyone be quiet," ordered Ray as they approached.

"Yes, Sir!" replied George in a booming voice.

"Shhh! Keep it down," said Jake.

Like a herd of buffalo they entered the dark tent, bumping into things and talking way too loud. Forgetting to duck when he entered, Jake hit his head with a loud clang on one of the metal supports. "Ouch! Damn it!" he said rubbing his head.

"Hey, you guys shut up," came a voice from one of the soldiers that had been awoken. "Some of us are trying to sleep."

"Ok, everyone to bed," ordered Ray.

"Hold on, I gotta pee," said Joe.

"Me too," said George and Jake, at the same time.

After relieving themselves, they made it to their beds. A moment later, Joe sprang up. "I think I'm gonna be sick," he said as he ran for the exit.

"Oh hell," said George.

"Keep it down, damn it," said another soldier.

A second later the sounds of violent vomiting filled the tent. Ray lay on his cot listening to George, the world spinning, and for a moment he thought he might have to follow Joe outside, but the nausea passed. Joe bumped his way back in a few minutes later.

"I feel a lot better," he said as he fell onto his cot like a dead man.

"Go to sleep," said Ray, groggily. "You're gonna need it, you have a fight tomorrow."

Jake and George had already passed out and Chuck was laughing at the situation.

Cody was suddenly brought back to reality when he heard his grandfather walking down the hallway. Quickly he slid the journal under his blanket and grabbed his book.

"You getting hungry yet?" asked his grandfather as he came into the room.

"Yeah, I could go for some lunch."

"Alright then, let's get over to Rosie's; they have some lunch specials that are pretty good."

Returning home from Roseys after a satisfying meal the rain had started to come down hard. With little hope of any outdoor activities Ray put on a movie and got comfortable in his recliner. Cody headed straight back into his room and pulled out the diary, continuing where he left off.

Ray awoke slowly like a man emerging from a thick grey fog. The first hint of reality was the throbbing pain of a hangover hammering away on the inside of his skull. Bleary eyed he glanced down at his wristwatch. It was nearly 10 o'clock. And then he suddenly remembered that Joe had a boxing match at 11:00 a.m. sharp. Sitting up he nearly fell out of bed but caught his balance. Glancing over he saw Chuck reading a newspaper that he had bought back in town. Painfully he thought, *how can he read it? It's in French.* Joe, George and Jake were still asleep. Otherwise the barracks were empty.

In a raspy voice, Ray said, "We need to get Joe up; he's got a fight in an hour."

"Go right ahead," replied Chuck. "Last time I woke him after a night of drinking, he nearly flattened me." A little smile spread across Ray's face as he remembered the incident.

"Ok, I'll do it," said Ray at the same time massaging his temples with the hope that it would help alleviate his headache. His brain then registered a dull pain from his left arm. He looked down at the fresh tattoo, dried blood and slightly swollen skin and thought *what the hell was I thinking?* His attention was then drawn over to Jake.

"Oh my head," said the big man, slowly rising from his cot and looking half dead. He squinted at the bright light coming through the tent opening and with a groan laid back down covering his head with his blanket.

Ray walked over to Joe's cot and gave him a shake. "Joe, get up, you got a fight this morning."

Without warning Joe sat straight up. "Fight!? Where!?"

"Calm down," said Ray taking a step back just in case Joe started swinging. Just as quickly, Joe lay back down with a weak moan and put his pillow over his head.

"Come on, Dempsey, you have to get up."

"No, I'm not fighting today," came his muffled voice from under the pillow. "I'm gonna sleep. Go away."

Ray stood for a moment considering how best to handle the situation. He knew that arguing with Joe wasn't going to work and he didn't have enough time to let him sleep his hangover off. He also knew if Joe didn't make the fight he would never live it down and never forgive Ray. And no matter the excuse, he would be looked at as a coward by the men. *Desperate times call for desperate measures,* he thought. Ray turned and walked over to Jake just out of earshot from Joe and whispered in the big man's ear.

"He's gonna be pissed," said Jake.

"It's ok," replied Ray. "Just do it."

With a groan Jake got out of bed and slipped his boots on. He was a little unsteady at first and it took a second for his alcohol-soaked brain to adjust. Quietly he made his way over to Joe and stood towering over his sleeping form. He shot Ray a worried look. Ray nodded and whispered, "Go ahead."

Jake then looked over at Chuck, who had an amused look on his face. With a shrug, he said, "Ok, Sir, here goes." In one smooth motion Jake yanked the covers off and lifted Joe as if he weighed little more than a child; tossing him over his shoulder like a sack of grain.

"Hey, put me down you big dope!" Joe hollered. Struggling violently like an animal caught in a trap he tried to escape but Jake's giant-like strength was unbreakable.

All the commotion roused George who rolled out of bed and landed on the floor with a thud and a moan. Confused and still half-drunk he grabbed his boots. "Hey, wait up, where you guys going?"

Jake headed outside at a fast trot to a row of showers. Pulling aside a wrinkly curtain he turned one of the handles to full blast. A stream of ice cold water rained down. Kicking and screaming he forced Joe under the torturous water and held him there. Never before had Ray heard Joe unleash such a foul-mouthed tirade of profanity. Unable to break free, Joe was quickly soaked but eventually relented his struggle, "Ok, ok I'm awake!" he screamed. His freckled face, which was a pink hue most of the time, was glowing a bright red from the heat of his anger. Jake released his grip and quickly took a step back. He had seen Joe flatten too many guys and didn't want to get socked. Shivering, Joe stepped out of the shower. With his red hair dripping and clothing completely drenched he looked like a dog that had been left out in the rain. A second later one of the fellows from the crowd that had gathered tossed him a towel.

Back in the tent Ray was busy helping Joe put on his hand wraps. "Ok, we don't have much time," he said.

"Oh, hell I'm in no condition to fight," replied Joe.

Ray grinned but could tell from Joe's bloodshot eyes that he wasn't kidding.

"I told you to take it easy last night."

"Yeah, I remember, Sir, kind of."

"Ouch!" said Joe when Ray accidently bumped his still tender tattoo while tying on his gloves.

"I definitely remember getting that," he said, looking at the fresh ink.

Although the cold shower had awakened Joe's dazed brain somewhat he was still feeling the effects of last night's debauchery. Dehydrated, he sat chugging water and did his best not to be sick.

"You guys almost ready?" came Chuck's voice from the tent opening. "The natives are getting restless."

"Ten minutes," answered Ray as he finished tying the strings on Joe's gloves.

"You ready?" asked Ray.

"Yeah," said Joe weakly, taking another long drink of water.

"Ok, let's warm up."

Rising from his seat on shaky legs, Joe shadow boxed for five minutes; dancing around throwing combinations and bobbing and weaving while Ray ran a stopwatch.

"Time! Good, how do you feel?" asked Ray.

"Like crap, Sir."

"And you look like it, too. Just kidding," said Ray with a grin.

"Come on, let's get out there before they come in here and drag you out."

Joe took one last drink of water and followed Ray outside.

Fifty yards behind the tents in a grass covered field was the makeshift boxing ring. It had been put together with four long tent poles hammered deep into the ground at each corner and some rope. A large group of G.I's sitting on gas cans, ammo boxed and wooden supply crates surrounded the ring.

As Joe and Ray approached the ring a loud cheer went up. Ray lifted the top rope; ducking under it Joe tripped on the bottom rope and stumbled into the ring. The fumbling entrance brought a roar of laughter from the crowd. A wooden ammo crate acting as a stool awaited him in his designated corner where George, Chuck and Jake had already gathered.

Dropping heavily onto the crate he looked across the ring where his rival stood talking to one of his corner men. A little taller than Joe and covered in smooth lean muscles; Frank glanced over and gave him a smile that dripped with arrogance. Returning the stare with his best tough guy look, Joe growled, "I hate that guy." Joe and Frank were the two best boxers in the Battalion and had sparred several times. Each time they had gotten into the ring their exhibitions had turned into full-fledged brawls. Adding fuel to the fire was the fact that Joe was Irish and Frank was Italian, it was a natural rivalry that had been festering for months. Finally, after their last sparring match Frank challenged Joe for the Battalion championship; Joe eagerly accepted.

Both fighters were called to the center of the ring and given their instructions by referee, Private First Class Eddie Donavan. With an accent that was straight from New York he said: "I want a clean fight from the both of you's guys, ya hear me? Any funny business and I'll disqualify ya's. Do I make myself clear?" Locked in a fierce stare-down both men nodded in agreement. "Ok then, let's get it on." A second later they returned to their respective corners.

"Ok, now listen," said Ray as he inserted Joe's mouthpiece. "He's going to come out fast, so be ready for him."

"Yes Sir," replied Joe.

A second later a large cow bell that was borrowed from one of the local farmers clanged loudly. "Kick his ass, Dempsey!" shouted George as Joe raised his dukes and went to meet his opponent. Like Ray had predicted, Rizzo came charging out of his corner in a semi-crouch throwing bombs. Covering up quickly, Joe was battered by combinations of lefts and rights; the pain of the blows adding to the throbbing in his already aching head. Off balance and queasy, Joe did his best to cover up and avoid Rizzo's blows by bobbing and weaving. The crowed, fired up with the blistering start, was on its feet cheering. By the midpoint of the round Rizzo was in command and battering Joe around the ring. Fighting back in spurts and on the verge of being sick, Joe managed to catch Frank with a couple of hard right hands. Undaunted by Joe's blows and with a snarl on his face Frank kept up his two-fisted shellacking. Just moments before the round ended, he caught Joe with a blow to the stomach that sent the air whistling from his mouth and followed with an upper cut that sent him skidding across the ground.

"Get up, Dempsey!" yelled Ray.

"Come on Joe, get up!" hollered Jake.

Up at eight, Joe swayed unsteady, a trickle of blood coming from his nose. Rizzo, admiring his handiwork, stood laughing from his corner. A second later the bell clanged.

"Alright," said Ray as Joe flopped onto his box breathing hard. Wiping the blood from Joe's nose, Ray could see that his friend was nearly finished. Speaking deliberately, he said, "Look at me. Here is what you're going to do."

Just then George piped in. "Joe, he's kicking your ass, step it up will ya."

With a venomous look, Joe retorted angrily, "I'm doing the best I can; you want to come in here and give it a try?"

"Sit down, George! That's an order!" yelled Ray.

"Yes, Sir," said George, returning to his seat.

Turning his attention back to Joe, Ray said, "Listen up. Every time that bastard throws his left jab he drops it when he brings it back, leaving his chin wide open. Next time he throws it I want you to nail him hard with your right hand, right down the center. I want you to time him, ok?" Joe shook his head indicating that he understood.

With a loud gong the second round began. Rizzo, full of confidence bolted from his corner like a wild man, hell bent on knocking Joe's head off. Coming in low he telegraphed a wide left hook that Joe barely ducked under. Backing off from his rampaging opponent Joe waited for the opening he was looking for. Ducking another wild swing Frank then shot out a stiff jab. Seeing his opportunity, Joe countered with a hard right hand that caught Frank flush on the jaw followed by a left hook that snapped Rizzo's head. Dazed, he wobbled and fell to the ground where he sat for a few seconds shaking his head to clear the cobwebs. The crowd was on its feet screaming.

"That's it, Dempsey!" shouted Ray. "That's it!"

With the cocky smile knocked from his face, Frank climbed to his feet. Cleared to continue by the referee, Rizzo waded back in. Re-energized by the knockdown, Joe met Frank's attack with a determined look on his face and the two exchanged a whirlwind of leather in the center if the ring. Backing off a few steps, Joe again waited for the right time to strike. Coming in low Frank shot out a snapping jab. Joe made no attempt to block or avoid the blow but instead bit down hard on his mouthpiece and took the punch. And at the moment Rizzio brought his hand back Joe stepped in with a smashing right that carried the last of his waning strength. The punch exploded off Frank's jaw with an audible thud. The crowd winced at the sound. Stunned, Frank stumbled across the ring like a kid on roller skates for the first time and fell flat on his back; his eyes rolling into the back of his head. Out cold there was no need for a count, instead the referee waved the fight off and raised Joe's hands in victory as the crowd went berserk with loud cheers mixed with equally loud boos from Frank's fans.

Back in his corner Joe grabbed Ray by the shoulders to steady himself as everyone gathered around and congratulated him.

"Can I go back to bed now, Sir?" asked the exhausted fighter.

"Absolutely," said Ray with a big smile.

Resting on his cot Ray looked up as Private Daniels approached. "Sir, the Colonel wants to see you in his briefing tent, right away."

"Ok," said Ray. He followed Daniels as they made their way through camp. Curious, Ray asked, "Did the Colonel say what it was about?"

"No, Sir," answered Daniels. "Just that it was urgent."

Colonel Schneider looked up as Ray entered the tent. "Please, close the flaps," said the Colonel. Ray turned and zipped the flap. Everyone in camp knew that when the tent flaps were closed the Colonel had serious business with someone or was about to handout a major ass chewing.

"Have a seat, Lieutenant."

"Yes, Sir."

"I received a letter this morning from London, directly from General Barrack."

The name instantly caught Ray's attention. Everyone knew of James Barrack, the fearless, flamboyant general that was leading the fight across the European Theatre.

"Must be serious," said Ray.

"It is," replied the Colonel.

"I have been ordered to gather a group of six men for a top secret mission. I believe that you are the man to assemble and lead that group. You have one hour to put together a team and meet me back here for further briefing."

Ray sat for a moment. "Yes Sir," he said as he got up.

"Oh and by the way," said the Colonel. "You're being promoted to Captain."

The news was a big surprise that brought a smile to Ray's face. "Thank you, Sir," he said as he exited the tent.

Chapter Seven
England

An hour later, Ray and his team stood assembled before Colonel Schneider. "At ease, gentlemen," said the Colonel. The fellows relaxed a little. As ordered, Ray had put together a team that included Joe, Jake, George, Chuck and fellow 5th Battalion member Larry Thorn. Larry was a rugged soldier as tough as a piece of dried leather and an excellent marksman. He didn't talk much, preferring to be monosyllabic, but had proven his courage by fighting alongside Ray and the fellows in several major battles.

"As Ray may or may not have told you there is a mission that you men have been selected for. I don't have a lot of info, so I hope you don't have a lot of questions. All I can tell you is that you will be leaving here shortly and flown to London where you will meet up with General Barrack." The men glanced at each other at the mention of the General's name.

"Must be a hell of a mission to have Barrack involved," said George.

"From what little I was told, it is," replied the Colonel. "So if you're ready follow me."

Schneider led Ray and his men to a tarp covered transport truck affectionately called a "Deuce-and-a-half," that was waiting outside.

"They're going to drive you to the airfield and fly you over to London. I want to wish each of you good luck," said the Colonel shaking each of their hands in turn. "I don't know if you will be coming back here once your mission is completed, but I want to say it has been an honor to have served with each of you men."

Standing before Schneider, Ray gave him a firm handshake; he had always liked the Colonel.

"Good luck, Ray."

"Same to you, Sir." And for a moment as their eyes locked Ray got the strange feeling that he would never see the Colonel again. Ray then turned and tossed his duffel bag up to Jake and climbed aboard. A second later the truck jerked forward with a grinding of gears and roared away.

"So what do you think this mission is all about?" asked Jake.

"Don't know," answered Ray.

"Well it must be pretty damn important," said Chuck, "to have the top brass like General Barrack involved."

"You ain't kiddi'n," said Joe.

Fifteen minutes later the truck came to a stop at the runway with a squeaking of brakes. Climbing out of the bed Ray was met by two saluting pilots.

"Afternoon, Captain," said a tall, lanky fellow. "My name is Phil, this here is Dale."

"How you doing, Sir?" asked Dale.

"Just fine," answered Ray.

It was just then that Phil and Dale were struck speechless as their attention was drawn to Jake climbing out of the truck bed.

"Is that Jake Cutter the football player?" asked Phil in an ecstatic tone. "I heard he was here in France."

"Yeah, that's him," said Ray with a smile, "in the flesh."

"Wow!" said Dale excitedly, "can I get a picture and an autograph, Sir?"

"Sure, but let's make it quick," replied Ray.

"Ok, thank you, Sir, I'll be right back," he said as he sprinted at top speed back to the plane to grab his camera and a pen.

"Hi," said Jake flashing his crooked smile as he and the rest of the men came walking up.

With a look of delight Phil stammered nervously, "It's nice to meet you, Jake. I'm a big fan," he said shaking Jake's enormous hand. A second later, Dale ran up huffing and puffing.

"Hi, Jake, mind if I get a picture with you?"

"Not at all," replied the big man.

Handing his camera to Ray, Dale and Jimmy stood next to Jake smiling hugely, their heads barley reaching up to Jake's massive shoulders. Ray clicked off a few pictures and handed the camera back to Dale. "Thanks," said Dale, smiling. "I can't wait to get these developed."

Larry, amused by the attention Jake was getting, asked Ray. "This happen often?"

"All the time," answered Ray.

Strapped into the seats of the Douglas C-47, Ray and the fellows prepared for takeoff.

"You guys ready?" hollered Jimmy from the cockpit, the noise of the idling engines nearly drowning out his voice. Ray gave Jimmy the thumbs up signal; a moment later the dual engines throttled up with a roar up and the plane began to move. Looking over, Ray could see that George was nervous. He knew that George hated flying; his knuckles were white as he clutched his seatbelts.

"You ok, George?" shouted Ray.

George gave Ray an annoyed look. "You know I hate flying, Sir." He then closed his eyes as the plane began to rise from the runway. Smiling to himself, Ray wondered how George could fight across half of Europe and rarely show fear, but turn into a nervous wreck when it came to flying in a perfectly safe plane.

"Don't worry, George," said Chuck, "it's only an hour flight."

"That's an hour too long for me," growled George.

Once the plane reached cruising altitude and leveled off Ray and the rest of the fellows relaxed a little, but not George. He continued to maintain a tight grip on his straps and looked as if he was on the verge of panicking every time the plane shook from even the slightest turbulence.

"How you guys doing?" asked Dale as he emerged from the cockpit.

"Fine," replied Ray.

"Hey, who's flying the damn plane?" snapped George.

"Oh, don't worry," answered Dale, "Phil's got the controls."

"We'll be in London shortly, Sir. They radioed to let us know that you will be met at the base by Major General Bill Burn and Field Marshal Basil Edmonds."

"Sounds good," said Ray with a nod.

"Field Marshal Sir Basil Edmonds?" asked Joe in a voice that resonated his excitement. "The Basil Edmonds? This is definitely serious, he's the supreme leader of the entire British Army and second only to Winston Churchill."

"Not to mention, he's also head of the British Secret Intelligent Services," said Chuck.

Just then Jake turned to Ray and asked, "What the hell have we gotten ourselves into, Sir?"

With a stern look Ray replied, "I don't know, big man, but I'm sure we're gonna find out."

A little over an hour later the plane touched down smoothly, much to the relief of George. Ray and his team could see two green "Willy's" jeeps and two men, one wearing an American Army uniform, the other a British uniform. Both were puffing heavily on cigarettes. With help from Dale and Phil the fellows unloaded their belongings and bid the pilots farewell.

Standing before the two senior officers Ray and his team saluted. With a return salute the man in the American uniform spoke. "Good afternoon, Captain Miller, I'm Major General Bill Burns." Burns looked to be about fiftyish and sported a graying flattop haircut and neatly trimmed mustache. His face was round and fleshy and his smile was friendly. "This gentleman standing next to me is an Air Marshal Sir Basil Edmonds of the Royal British Army."

The man was tall and straight, with a pointy chin and nose, close cropped brown hair and intelligent brown eyes. "It's certainly a pleasure to meet you gentlemen," said Basil with a precise English accent and a friendly smile. "I trust your flight was comfortable."

"It was," replied Ray, shooting a glance over to George who returned the look with an angry frown. The men then shook hands all around and exchanged pleasantries.

Shaking Jake's hand both Basil and Bill were visibly impressed with the football player's mountainous size. "I'm a big fan of yours," remarked the Major.

"Thanks, Sir," replied Jake modestly.

"You're bigger than I expected," continued Burns. "Maybe, if we have some time later, we can talk a little football."

"I'd like that, Sir," said Jake.

With introductions out of the way everyone piled into the jeeps. Following a quick drive across the base Ray and the fellows were shown to the barracks by Sir Basil. "I trust these quarters will be adequate, Captain." The barracks, housed in a large two story building were clean and neat, a far cry from the damp, dirt floor tent that Ray and his men had been living in.

"They'll do just fine," said Ray dropping his duffel bag onto one of the cots.

"Go ahead and get unpacked," said Bill. "General Barrack has a meeting set up for us at 1800 hours. That gives you fellas a few hours to get settled in."

"Thank you, Sir," said Ray saluting as Burns and Edmonds left.

With some free time the fellows chose their beds, unpacked and sat around talking about the mission and meeting. Two hours later Burns returned. "I see you fellas have made yourselves comfortable," he said as he walked into the barracks.

"Yes, Sir, we have," replied Ray, he and the guys jumping up and standing at attention.

"Well, then if you're ready, I will walk you over to the briefing room."

Burns led them across the base to a large building with armed guards at the front door. Down a long echoing hallway, and finally into a room that resembled a classroom, complete with chairs, desks and a large roll-around bulletin board. Placed to the left of the board was an American flag, to the right a British. "Please have seat, gentlemen, I'll get the General."

A few minutes later Burns returned with Basil and General Barrack. Instantly, Ray and the fellows stood at attention saluting the General. Returning the salute, Barrack said, "Be seated, men." Barrack was perhaps sixty-years-old with a clean shaved head, hard-lined facial features and piercing green eyes. A jagged white scar about six inches long ran from his left eyebrow down to the bottom of his cheek. The wound, compliments of a German knife, was acquired during a vicious hand-to-hand trench battle in World War One.

The General's military career, as everyone knew, had begun during World War One when he lied about his age and enlisted at the tender age of sixteen. From there he rose to prominence by impressing his superiors with his fearlessness in battle and his hard-driving and charismatic leadership abilities. At this point of his career the General was a living legend.

Standing before Ray and his team, Barrack gave them an intense look and then spoke in a deep voice. "Colonel Schneider assured me he would be sending the best men he had; well, by God, I hope he is right." After a brief pause he continued in a voice full of emotion. "Gentlemen, we're in a race, a race against the Germans to get the first Atomic Bomb and as of now we are losing that race."

At mention of the Atomic Bomb, Ray and his men were caught off guard. They had all heard bits of whispered rumors and speculations about the Germans and Allies trying to build a bomb so powerful that just one could destroy a major city. But, up to this point, Ray had thought that it was just talk. He had no idea that the Germans were close to perfecting a weapon powerful enough to bring America and the Allied Forces to their knees. His attention was then drawn back to the General. "If the Germans succeed in developing an Atomic weapon and unleashing it on American soil we will lose this war." Turning the bulletin board around the fellows saw that it was covered in photographs. The General continued. "That's where you men come in. The United States and England have been working together for over a year to discover the secret location of the Hydroelectric Plant where the Germans are producing hard-water and Plutonium necessary to build Atomic Bombs. As of now we have located the plant." Barrack then pointed out dozens of aerial and ground level pictures of a compound consisting of a large two-story building and two smaller ones. The buildings were surrounded by an eight foot reinforced concrete wall topped with barbed wire. Several other photos were of Germans in uniforms and what appeared to be scientists in long lab coats.

"We have found that not only are the Germans making hard-water here, but we also believe that two bombs, that are nearly completed, are being assembled here as well. The project is being overseen by one of Hitler's top Generals, you may have heard of him." Using a long wooden pointer Barrack pointed to a picture of a man in a black uniform. The man was handsome with strong German features; it was his eyes however that betrayed him. Dark and brooding, they reflected the evil that lurked within his wicked soul. "Eric Von Richten," said the General, "also known as, 'The Hound of the

Reich.'" The very utterance of the name was like a blasphemous curse. Tense glances were shared. Everyone had heard of him. "The Hound" was known as Hitler's most ruthless and sadistic general. Stories were told by soldiers about the thousands of Jews Von Richten had been responsible for executing. Other stories circulated about how he had personally and without mercy killed hundreds of Jewish and Polish prisoners, including women and children. And that "The Hound" was particularly fond of torturing Allied prisoners to death.

"Von Richten has headed up this project for the last two years and is using every available resource to get those bombs completed, that's why it's critical that we stop him now." Pausing for a moment the General's voice sank low. "If given the chance you are to kill that son-of-a-bitch by any means necessary, do I make myself clear?"

"Yes Sir," said Ray and his team in unison.

The General then gave each of then a hard look. "Make no mistake; if you are captured he will kill each and every one of you."

Pausing for several seconds Barrack suddenly spoke passionately. "Men, the fate of the free world hangs in the balance. And the lives of millions of innocent people are depending on you. We must stand up to the might of the Nazi war machine and we must be victorious. We are putting our trust and our hope in you that you will succeed in blowing up that facility and putting an end Hitler's dreams of world domination." For a moment he paused and let out his breath. "Before I turn the floor over to Sir Basil, I want you to remember one thing. Years from now when you're old and grey and your grandchildren are sitting on your lap you'll be thankful that you had the guts to stand up and face the enemy head-on and win. That is all I have to say." With that the General took a seat.

"Thank you, General," said Basil as he made his way to the front of the room. "From here I would like to go over the plan we have come up with and answer any question or concerns you might have. Five days from now you will fly a Waco glider into Germany, and land it near Berlin at a predesignated drop zone where you will meet up with one of our top agents." Basil pointed to the picture of a man in a coat and hat. There was little doubt, judging from his features, that he was German. "This is Hans Schmitt. He is the leader of an anti-Nazi resistance group of rebels and a trusted ally. After you land you will rendezvous with Hans. He will equip you with the necessary explosives to destroy the plant. He will also help you gain entrance into the compound. Once inside, you will place timed explosives on the electrolysis chambers that contain the hard-water." Basil then pointed to several photographs of long stainless steel cylindrical tubes lined up in rows, perhaps six feet tall and three feet in diameter. "After the charges are set you will leave the plant and meet up with Hans at a train station that is located about five miles from the building. From there you will board the train and ride it into a liberated section of Poland where you will be met by Allied agents. During the next five days we will go over this plan in much greater detail. But for now are there any questions you would like to ask?"

To the surprise of Ray and the rest of the fellows Larry spoke up. "I have one, Sir. Why not just drop a couple of 500 pound bombs on the place and be done with it?"

"That's a good question," responded Basil. "Initially we thought about a bombing run. But because the plant is near a large city we don't want to endanger innocent civilians in the event that one of the bombs misses its target. After a lengthy discussion with General Barrack we both agreed that an aerial bombing is our absolute last option."

Larry shook his head in understanding.

"Are there any further questions?"

The fellows looked at each other. Ray then answered, "None at this time, Sir."

"Very well, we will continue tomorrow outlining the mission, which we have code-named operation Night Hawk, in greater detail, and begin preparations for your departure."

Wow, thought Cody as he finished the page. *This is like something out of a movie.* In anticipation he turned the page eager to read about operation Night Hawk, only to find that it was blank.

"What?" he said out loud in a disbelieving tone. He quickly flipped through the next few pages; like the previous ones they were all blank. In fact, the rest of the journal was blank. *You have got to be kidding me*, he thought closing the journal. Lying there, his mind raced through several different thoughts. *Maybe the mission never happened. Maybe that's why the journal is blank.* He immediately dismissed that thought. *There's no way. If it never happened he would have written it down. Maybe it was so top secret that he was sworn to secrecy and wasn't allowed to keep a record.*

Finally, Cody concluded that there was only one way to find out; he had to ask his grandfather. The boy thought about marching out and confronting his grandpa, but he was too afraid. He recalled how his grandfather had reacted when he'd asked about George losing his leg. He then thought about asking one of the guys at the donut shop, except how would he get to them without his grandfather being around? His thoughts then shifted to Joe and the ten-speed bicycle and he remembered that his grandfather had a doctor's appointment tomorrow morning at 10:00. That would mean that Cody and his grandfather would go to the donut shop and come back home for a while. His grandfather would then go to his appointment and Cody would have just enough time to bike over to Joe's house and get back before his granddad returned.

With his plan worked out Cody made up his mind. Tomorrow morning, after his grandfather went to see his doctor, he would ride to Joe's house and ask him about the secret mission and about Jake.

Having returned from the donut shop Cody sat anxiously watching TV and sipping the last of his hot chocolate while his grandfather prepared to leave for his appointment. "I think I have everything," said Ray grabbing up his car keys, "I'll be back in an hour or so."

"Ok," said Cody.

Peeking from behind the front room curtains Cody watched his grandfather back out of the driveway and disappear down the street. He then darted into his room. Grabbing his backpack he placed the journal inside and snatched up his jacket. A few minutes later he was peddling down the street shifting the ten-speed into top gear. Looking skyward Cody could see that the clouds were dark and threatening rain; he hoped that he would make it to Joe's before it started pouring.

Twenty minutes later he pulled up to the front porch of Joe's house and the dogs once again swarmed him. Knocking on the front door Cody was greeted by Ellen. "Well, hi Cody, I'm surprised to see you. Where's your granddad?"

"He's not here, I came on my bike. Is Joe home?"

"Yes, he's out in the garage, would you like me to get him for you?"

"No, that's ok; I just need to ask him something."

"Ok, then," she said as Cody turned and headed for the garage.

Joe looked up from the broken fishing pole he was repairing when Cody entered the garage.

"Hi Joe," said Cody.

"Cody, I'm surprised to see you today. You come over for some more fishing?" Looking past the boy Joe inquired, "Where's your granddad?"

"He's at the doctor's, I rode my dad's old ten-speed over here," answered Cody.

"Doctor's, is he ok?

"Yeah, he's fine, just has a sore foot."

"Oh, that again," said Joe with a grin, "no wonder he didn't mention it this morning at the donut shop, he's been complaining about that for years." Cody could see that Joe looked relieved as he went back to reattaching the eye that had broken off from the fishing pole he was working on.

"So, what brings you here, young man?"

Cody stammered for a moment, a bit of nervousness running through his body. "I, uh, I have a question to ask you."

"Go right ahead, kid," said Joe, concentrating intently while he wrapped a tight line of fine thread around the fishing pole.

"Was your nickname, Dempsey?"

At the mention of the name Joe stopped as if turned to stone and a faraway look came to his eyes. For a few seconds he seemed to be remembering things long ago forgotten. "Well, that's a name I haven't heard in a long, long time." Joe then leveled a questioning look at Cody. "Who told you that my nickname was Dempsey? Was it your granddad?"

"No," answered the boy. Cody then pulled off his backpack, unzipped it and withdrew the journal. "I read it in here."

At the sight of the old journal, Joe's eyes widened in astonishment and his normally happy expression disappeared. "I haven't seen that since 1945. Thought your grandfather threw it away a long time ago. Does he know you have it?"

"No way," answered the boy.

"It's probably better that he doesn't," replied Joe.

"I read the whole thing," explained Cody. "All about how you guys fought at Normandy and how you got your tattoos and about Jake."

At the mention of Jake, Joe's eyes flashed to Cody's and the boy could tell that he was treading on dangerous ground. Swallowing hard he continued. "And I read about a secret mission that you guys were part of, at least the beginning. The rest of it is not in here. I want to know what happened on the mission and I want to know about Jake."

Joe sat for a moment without saying a word. Finally he spoke. "You want to know about the mission and about Jake? You're going to have to ask your grandfather."

"Ask my grandfather, no way," said Cody, visibly crestfallen. "He won't talk about it. He'll just get mad."

"Well, I'm sorry but if you want to know the rest of the story you're going have to talk to him."

Cody could tell by the tone of Joe's voice that he wasn't going to get the answers he so desperately wanted.

"Can I at least ask you one thing?"

"Sure," replied Joe.

"What happened to him? Why is he the way he is? You know, never smiling and kind of sad."

Again Joe sat silent for several moments before answering. When he did it was in a voice that was tinged with sorrow. "Something happened in the war that changed him, something he's carried inside of him for fifty-years; a pain that has eaten at his soul. We've all tried to talk to your granddad over the years about what happened but none of us have been able to reach him." After a reflective pause Joe continued. "That war took a lot out of every one of us, but it took the most from your granddad." Giving Cody a meaningful look Joe continued. "He needs you, Cody. He needs you before it's too late, if you get my meaning." Cody shook his head not really grasping, at the moment, the full meaning of Joe's words. "Now, you better get home before the rain starts."

"Ok, Joe, I'll see you tomorrow at the donut shop."

Later that evening Cody sat in his room agonizing about how best to approach his grandfather. He had already made up his mind that there was no way he was going back home without hearing the rest of the story. Sitting on his bed he kept staring at the picture of his grandfather and his pals, his eyes always returning to Jake's smiling face. It was then that Cody heard Joe's voice resonate in his mind. "He needs you, Cody. He needs you before it's too late." He then grasped the full meaning of those words. His thoughts returned to the morning when he first found the journal. Then it hit him. What he had felt that morning while holding the Medal of Honor was Jake's spirit and it was full of pain; the same pain his grandfather now carried.

Cody knew what he had to do. Deliberately the boy picked up the journal and stood up. Holding it, his hand shook a little as a wave of nervousness coursed through his body. The only time he could remember being this anxious was when he had to give a speech on the Civil War in front of his class. Clenching his jaw resolutely he stepped out of his room and headed down the hallway.

In the front room he found his grandfather perusing his library of old movies.

"Grandpa?"

"Yeah?" replied Ray fixated on looking through the large collection.

"I have something to tell you."

With his glasses low on his nose Ray looked over at Cody. "What is it?"

Suddenly, Cody felt warm all over and could feel sweat beading his forehead. In a shaky voice that betrayed his nervousness he held out the journal and said, "I, I read this."

Ray looked down at the journal and took it from Cody's hand, his eyes flashing with anger. Cody shrank back from the force of his grandfather's gaze. In a booming voice he said, "You had no right to read this! No right at all!"

More scared than he had ever felt in his life, the boy replied, "I know, but, but I need to know about the mission and about," Cody paused for a second before saying the name. "Jake."

"You don't need to know a damn thing!" snapped Ray. Turning away for a second he fought to get control of his rising anger.

Nearly overcome with anxiety, Cody dug deep and found the courage to speak up. "Grandpa, you need to talk about this. I talked to Joe today while you were at the doctor's. You have carried it around for too long. And I need to know what happened."

Deep down Ray knew that his grandson was right. And he had always known that this day would come; the day when he would have to confront the pains of his past. A moment later he turned back around and faced his grandson. Looking at the boy, Ray thought about how much Cody resembled him when he was sixteen. His anger slowly subsided.

"Sit down." It was an order, not a request. Cody took a seat on the couch and sat silent and unmoving. Ray took a seat in his recliner placing the journal on his lap.

"You want to know about Jake and the mission?" Cody shook his head yes. Ray looked down at the aged journal resting on his lap. With a deep breath he took off his glasses and placed them on the table next to the recliner. And for the first time in fifty years he spoke of Jake and Operation Night Hawk.

"Jake," he began in a calm voice, "was my best friend, my brother really. You see, Jake was an orphan. His dad was a drunk and ran off not too long after he was born and Jake's mom was killed in a car wreck when he was nine. With no relatives or family to take him in, my parents, your great grandparents, agreed to watch him for a time. Well, eventually he just became part of the family and they raised us together. After high school Jake went to college in Cincinnati on a scholarship and I drove trucks with Joe. After a couple of years in college Jake started playing professional football and was eventually picked up by the Cincinnati Bullies. With his great strength and God given abilities he became one of the best players in the country and a national superstar.

Of course all of this came crashing down on December 7, 1941 when the Japanese attacked us at Pear Harbor. It was a few days after the attack that I joined the Army. I was 24-years-old at the time. It didn't take long for Joe, George and Chuck to join me; we had all been friends since we were kids and even when we grew up we were nearly inseparable. It was a few days later that Jake showed up from Cincinnati. I tried to talk him out of joining because I was worried that something might happen to him, but he was hell-bent on fighting for his country. He always was patriotic. 'To hell with football,' he said, 'it's just a game. This is our country and our homes we're talking about.'" Ray paused for a moment in reflective thought. Cody sat unmoving, riveted to the story. And then Ray continued.

"As you know from reading my journal we were flown over to London where we met up with General Barrack and Air Marshal Basil Edmonds. I don't need to tell you that after hearing about Operation Night Hawk and Atomic Bombs the fellas and I were more than a little worried."

Hardly daring to breathe, Cody sat listening as his grandfather began recounting the events where the journal left off; events that changed the very course of world history.

Back at the barracks Ray and the fellows sat talking about the mission. "I don't like it," said George. "Seems like a one way ticket to suicide if you ask me." It was easy to tell that George was upset about having to fly in a glider. "They actually expect us to fly a glider into Germany. You know, they call those things 'canvas coffins.' And the guys who fly them 'suicide jockeys.'" Ray sat silent. He knew that it was good to let the fellows talk things out.

"I still can't believe it," said Joe, "all the talk, all the rumors, they're all true. The Nazis are building Atomic bombs; this is a lot more serious than I thought." He then looked over at Chuck. "So Chuck, what do you think?"

Chuck sat silent for a moment before answering. "I think George is right. It's extremely dangerous. The odds of us pulling it off are slim at best."

"I can't believe you guys," said Jake, standing up from his cot. They all looked up at the big man. "For the last two years we've been through Hell fighting all over Europe and now you're gonna sit here and whine likes a bunch of sissies. You heard General Barrack, if the Nazis get that bomb operational we're not going to have a home to go back to. There will be no more America and a lot of innocent people are going to die." He paused for a moment and took a deep breath. "I for one think we can do it." He looked over at Ray. "A lot of people are depending on us. Not just back home, but all over the world."

Ray sat quiet for a while mulling his thoughts over. He didn't like the idea of being dropped off in the middle of enemy territory, and left to complete a mission that was so top secret only a handful of people would even know they were there. He knew Chuck and George were right. The odds were stacked against them. But, he also knew that Jake was right. Somebody had to stop the Germans.

Ray spoke up and everyone else stopped talking. "I think we've talked about this long enough. We all know that this is a dangerous assignment. But somebody has to do it." He paused and gave the fellows a long hard look. He knew he had to say something that would reassure them; give them something to believe in. "For the last two years we've tramped all over Europe and I've been the leader. In all that time I've never steered you wrong, and I won't do it now. I'll promise each of you one thing. I'll make sure that we all get back home, you hear me?" They all looked at Ray, not without worry in their eyes and nodded. "Good, now we have a mission to get ready for."

Ray knew that there was a good chance that he might not be able to keep his promise, but what more could he do? Besides, hadn't they already survived incredible odds making it this far and through so much.

The next five days were spent in intense training. Ray and his team, along with Basil and several members of the British Secret Intelligence went over the mission in great detail. They pored over aerial photograph of the hydro-plant and studied pictures of the building's interior lay-out. The photos, explained Basil, had been smuggled out of Germany by a scientist working at the plant, who was also an agent working for Hans.

Because it was essential that Ray and his men destroyed the correct tanks a special mock up building had been constructed complete with several hard-water tubes exactly like the ones in the photographs. Ray and the fellows ceaselessly practiced laying dummy charges and becoming familiar with where to place them for the greatest effect. They took part in drills to improve their speed and skill and spent time getting familiar with the components that the explosives used like fuses, detonators and wires.

During the early morning their training consisted of flying and landing their brown canvas covered Waco CG-4A glider. Each day a C-47 would pull the 80' wood and steel framed glider up by a nylon tow cable and release them. Because Larry already had extensive training and had flown and landed a glider on D-Day he was designated as the pilot. Ray, being the leader of the group was made co-pilot. Upon reaching the drop altitude, they would, under the directions of their instructor, glider the Waco back to Earth. Since they would be landing in the dark, several practice runs were done by night, but with the advantage of a lighted runway. In Germany they would only have the dim light of the moon and Hans, who would be using a flashlight and acting as their pathfinder. Landing at night intensified the danger ten-fold. Ray and his team knew that landing in enemy territory in the dark on an unfamiliar runway would be perilous; and there would be no second chances. They were, however, assured by Basil that Hans had picked out as safe a place as possible to land.

After five days of training, Ray and his team felt supremely confident that they could blow the Hydro-plant sky high. There was only one problem. They had not gone over a plan to gain entrance into the compound.

"Don't trouble yourself about that," said Edmonds. "Hans has assured me that he will have a fitting plan to get you inside the plant."

Later that evening Ray and his men stood ready to board their glider. The weather was agreeable and the conditions were optimal. Every man was dressed in a rugged army green uniform, high topped leather boots and helmet. Armaments were the finest weapons the military had to offer. Each of them, except Joe, carried an M1A1 Thompson submachine gun with two hundred and twenty rounds as well as a silencer equipped British Welrod pistol. Joe carried his Springfield sniper rifle, also fitted with a silencer as well as the Welrod. Each man also carried four fragment grenades and an 8" razor sharp KA-Bar knife. Because of the nature of the mission all of them had been given a suicide capsule, sewn into the collar of their uniform for quick access. The pill, once bitten into contained enough Cyanide to kill a man in just a few minutes.

Standing before the fellows, Edmonds, Burns and Barrack gave all of them a handshake and a salute and wished them good luck. "When this mission is over," said Barrack, "I will personally buy each of you a drink." To Jake he said, "I expect to have seats at the 50-yard line when you play your first return game."

"You can count on that, Sir," said Jake with a big grin.

A few minutes later they were loaded into the glider and strapped into the hard plywood seats. As usual George looked miserable and was holding on tight as the C-47 throttled up and began to move. With a tug the nylon line attaching the two aircraft was pulled tight and the glider began to roll. Ray and Larry watched in the moonlight as the big plane built up speed and lifted off. Trailing 350 feet behind it only took a second and then they too were airborne. The glider shook and bounced and the canvas skin slapped against the metal frame as they climbed into the star-lit sky.

Once they reached cruising altitude Larry lit up a cigarette with one hand while steering the glider with the other. Ray loaded his lip with a wad of chew and turned to his men. "I want you guys to check your equipment and make sure everything is ready for our landing."

"Yes, Sir Captain," said Jake with an extra emphasis on the "Captain" and a playful grin.

Sometime later Ray glanced down at his watch and saw that it was nearly time for release. The plane would release them and Ray and his team would glide down from 8,000 feet traveling several miles before landing. Flicking on his SCR-536 radio known among soldiers as a "Handie Talkie," he called to the pilots. A moment later a crackly voice responded. "How are you fellas doing back there, Captain Miller?"

Ray, still getting used to hearing "Captain" before his name, answered, "We're doing fine, just a little anxious."

"I hear you, Captain. We will be releasing in about five minutes."

Five minutes later the pilot's voice came back over the radio. "Ok, Captain, you ready?"

"We're all set," replied Ray. Looking over, Ray saw that Larry was sitting straight up gripping the controls with both hands.

"On my mark," came the pilot's voice. "3-2-1," a second later Ray pulled the release lever and the glider was on its own. By light of the moon Ray could see the C-47 bank left, the drone of its massive engines slowly fading as it headed back to London. A second later the pilot's voice came over the radio. "Good luck, boys."

Ray clicked the button on his radio and replied, "Thanks."

"Ok, guys, we're starting our descent. Larry, you know what to do."

With a nod, Larry put the glider's nose down into a gradual dive. George closed his eyes like a terrified kid on a roller coaster and held on to his wooden seat.

With the C-47 gone the glider drifted effortlessly in stealthy silence. The only sound was the flapping of its canvas skin as they descended through the wispy clouds that blocked out the star covered sky.

Several minutes later Ray checked his altimeter and compass; he could see that they were nearing their landing zone. "Everyone hold tight," announced Ray. "Keep your eye out for a signal light," said Ray.

"Yes, sir," replied Larry.

Approaching the ground Larry and Ray could see a moonlit field dotted with small trees. "Hey," said Larry looking a little concerned. "I thought they said Hans had a safe place for us to land."

A second later a flash of light shone brightly out of the darkness a few hundred yards ahead of them. "There!" said Ray pointing at the light. "That must be the signal."

"I see it," said Larry, gripping the steering wheel tight. With skill Larry guided the glider toward the light doing his best to dodge trees.

"Hang on, guys," came Ray's warning as they neared the field. A second later the glider hit the uneven ground with a bone rattling jolt and bounced before coming down hard. Shaking violently the glider sped across the field. Larry applied the brakes and attempted to steer the plane away from danger. Suddenly there was a crashing sound of splintering wood and tearing fabric.

"Oh, Hell!" grunted Larry. The right side wing had caught a tree and was torn clean off. This caused the glider to careen into a spin and slide sideways. Digging into the ground the landing gear and wheels bent under the glider and the entire aircraft lifted and threatened to roll over. Everyone grabbed hold of whatever they could and held on as the glider slammed back to the ground and came to an abrupt stop.

"Everyone ok?" asked Ray.

"I think we're all right," said Joe, looking around.

"Yeah, we're fine," said Jake.

"That's it!" said George unstrapping his shoulder belts in a fit of rage. "I am never getting on one of these God damned flimsy things again!"

Ray hid his smile from George as he peered through the cockpit window; he couldn't see much in the darkness except a few trees.

"Everyone out," he ordered. "Let's see if we're in the right spot."

With their weapons at the ready, cautiously they opened the side door and climbed out into the cool night. Instinctively they spread out, crouching noiselessly.

Suddenly, a German voice broke the silence of the night. "Captain Miller. It is I, Hans." From out of the darkness two men appeared like phantoms. One Ray recognized as Hans who was dressed in all black clothing with a beanie on his head. He was taller and leaner than his photo had suggested and looked every bit the secret agent. The other appeared to be an older fellow dressed as a commoner in denim overalls.

"I am glad you made it in one piece, Captain," said Hans with a smile as he extended his hand and introduced his companion as Marcel.

"I'm not sure that qualifies as one piece," replied Ray, glancing over at the wrecked glider.

Hans then directed his attention to Ray's men and greeted each one. Seeing Jake he quipped, "By God you are a big one." Jake just smiled.

Turning back to Ray, Hans said, "The first thing we have to do is get the glider into Marcel's barn."

"Good Idea," said Ray. "The faster we can get this thing out of plain sight the better I'll feel."

Seeing that Ray and his men looked a little anxious, Hans smiled. "Have no fear, Captain. We are safe for the moment and far from any German soldiers." Hans then turned to Marcel and gave him instructions in German. A second later Marcel headed towards the dark shape of a large barn.

"Marcel is going to bring some horses and we will drag the glider into the barn." Because of the damage to the wheels and landing gear the aircraft would not roll. "In the meantime we can gather the wreckage and get it into the barn," Hans added.

Several minutes later Marcel returned with two massive horses trailing long ropes and a lantern. In no time he had the horses attached to the glider. With a guttural command the horses began pulling the glider, their great muscles flexing and standing out. Marcel guided them as they dragged the wrecked craft the hundred yards to the barn. Following along, Ray and the fellows carried pieces of the wing and strips of canvas. With the right side wing broken off they were able to just get the glider to fit into the barn. Once inside the barn doors were shut and locked.

"What's going to happen to the glider?" asked Chuck.

"Marcel and his young sons will tear it down and burn it," answered Hans. "Now if you're ready we have a five mile walk to my cabin."

In silence and on the alert despite the reassurance that they were safe Ray and his team made the five mile trek in quick time. They followed behind Hans down a well-traveled dirt road, sticking close to the darkness of the trees in case they had to hide. Fortunately they didn't run into any nocturnal travelers.

It was nearing midnight when they approached the town of Amberg. Ray and the fellows could see the silhouettes of houses, barns and building outlined by the moonlight. From some of the houses soft lights could be seen shining from windows. Silent as shadows they followed Hans behind buildings and down pitch black alleyways until finally coming to the rear of a small, dark house. Hans rapped on a door four times. A moment later a female's inquisitive voice was heard. Hans responded in German and the door was opened. Illuminated in a faint light Ray could see the form of a young girl. "Quickly, everyone inside," said Hans.

With everyone in, the girl shut and locked the door. Ray and the fellows found themselves in a living room/dining area. Furnishing consisted of a plain wooden table, four chairs and a worn brown couch. The ceiling, built low, had Jake crouching to avoid wooden beams. A fire crackled in the fireplace and the room glowed with comforting warmth. Compared to the chill of the night air the room felt hot. Two hard-eyed men smoking cigarettes watched from the couch as Ray and the fellows piled their gear in a corner and took off their jackets.

"Please make your selves comfortable" said Hans. "I know there is not a lot of room, but we will manage." Ray, Joe, Jake and George grabbed chairs. Larry and Chuck found spots on the floor next to the fire.

Gesturing to the men sitting on the couch Hans introduced the first one as Carl and the second as Axel. "They are my good friends and members of the anti-Nazi resistance."

Both men were of average height and build with blond hair, light skin and blue eyes; it was plain to see that they were brothers. "Carl is a demolition expert and once served in the German military, He's the one who built the explosives that you will be using. Axel is a scientist. He has been to the Hydro Plant and has extensive knowledge of the facility's layout. He also has a plan to get into the building. And finally this is my wife Uta." Short and dark haired, Uta had stood by silently; she now smiled shyly. "She only speaks and understands a little English," added Hans as he put his arm around her waist and spoke to her in German. With a smile and a nod she went into the small kitchen and began pulling out jars and cans of food. "Uta is going to make us some food."

"Great," said Ray. They were all hungry and hadn't eaten since flying out of England.

Turning to Axel, Ray said, "I'm curious to hear about the plan you have to get us into the hydro-plant."

With a look of excitement Axel sat up and took a long drag of his cigarette. In English that was spoken well, but with a thick German accent, he said, "Absolutely, Captain Miller." The rest of the fellows stopped talking and began listening as Axel outlined the plan.

"Tomorrow night we will climb over the rear wall of the compound down by the river's edge. It is the safest area to attempt a breach. We will then enter into the main building through a door that will be left unlocked for us. Once we are inside we will capture the scientist on duty and then set the explosives."

"And how are we gonna manage to get over the wall?" asked George bluntly. "They're twelve feet high and topped with razor sharp barbed wire. We can't just fly over them."

"You are right," replied Axel, "that is why Carl and I have built a special ladder that can be assembled when we get to the Plant. With it we can climb over the wall after we cut the through the barbed wire."

"What about the guards in the towers, won't they see us?" asked Joe.

"No," replied Axel. "They are lax and sleeping most of the time. Besides, it's over 200 feet from the nearest tower and we will be well hidden in the dark. We also have another advantage; the noise of the river will cover any sounds we might make."

"Still sounds dangerous," said Ray.

"Yes, Captain, it is not without its risks, but it is the only way." Axel then gave Ray an intent stare and took a long drag off his cigarette. "You must trust me, Captain, it is the only way. The Germans are nearing the completion of hard-water. Once it is done they will have the last component they need to construct their Atomic bomb. That is why it is absolutely critical that we stop them now. If we do not the Allied forces will unleash a massive aerial assault on the plant and many innocent people will be killed. Now is the time, Captain. The Germans are confident and their guard is down. They believe that the fear of the Von Richten will keep them safe. They will never expect such a bold move."

"I have a question," said George. "How come you guys didn't put together a team and sabotage the plant your selves? Why fly us in all the way from London, just to plant a few bombs?"

Axel shot a glance at his brother who had sat silent smoking a cigarette during the conversation. He now spoke.

"Von Richten, that is the answer. No one is willing to cross 'The Hound of the Reich.'" Carl looked at his brother with an almost guilty look on his face. "It's not that we don't have brave men willing to fight. The men of the Nazi resistance have proven themselves to be nearly fearless and many have given their lives. But to cross the Hound means certain death, not only for that person but also their families. Axel and I have no family. Our parents were sent to a prison camp and murdered by the Nazis because they were Jewish, so we have nothing left to lose. Likewise, Hans has no family besides Uta. And by using American soldiers we can ensure that there will be no retaliation by the Nazis against innocent families."

George gave him a nod, indicating that he understood.

"Hope you are hungry," said Hans as he and Uta came into the front room handing out steaming bowls piled high with pan seared sausages, boiled potatoes and chunks of bread; eagerly they all dug in.

After eating, the group talked late into the night, going over details and asking questions. Eventually the need for sleep became overpowering and Ray knew that they all needed a good night's rest if they hoped to succeed.

Chapter Ten
The Hydro-Plant

Ray awoke slowly. The house was quiet and the fire had died down to a few glowing orange coals. Looking around he could see Carl and Axel covered in blankets asleep on the couch. The rest of the fellows were sprawled out on the front room floor with their jackets wrapped tightly about them, all except Jake. Sitting up, Ray noticed that the front door was open a little. Tossing his blanket aside Ray slipped on his boots and zipped up his jacket. Opening the front door he was greeted by the morning sunlight that was just starting to peek over the horizon. He found Jake seated on the front porch wrapped in a blanket. Looking up he smiled and said, "Morning."

Thinking it was odd that Jake was sitting alone Ray asked, "You ok?"

Jake didn't answer right away; instead he sat looking into the blue and orange glow of the early morning dawn as if he were looking right through it, as if he were seeing something Ray could not. "Are we gonna make it?" he asked.

Ray thought for a moment. "You're damn right we are," he said heartily. He then grabbed the big man's shoulder and gave it a squeeze.

Jake looked up at Ray. "I hope you're right."

Looking down at his friend Ray was a little concerned about the melancholy mood Jake seemed to be in; it wasn't like him at all.

"Besides," said Ray with a big grin that he hoped would help lift the dark mood, "what could possibly go wrong? We have the great Jake Cutter on our side. Now come on, let's get back inside before someone sees us."

After breakfast Ray and his men were led into a hidden basement under the house. It was here that Carl had constructed the timed explosives using an alarm clock as a trigger to set off the detonators. The clock was attached to a square two pound block of C-3 which in turn would be wired to twenty-five, two pound blocks.

"That's a lot of C-3," said Ray after seeing how much they were going to use.

"Definitely going to make a big boom," added Joe.

"Yes, it is, but necessary," replied Carl. "We want to make sure every tank in the building is completely destroyed."

Peeking over Ray's shoulder, Jake said, "Better make damn sure were nowhere near when that stuff blows."

Carl glanced up at Jake. "We won't be. As long as everything goes as planned we will be far out of range."

"As long as everything goes as planned," repeated George sarcastically as he looked over the large pile of explosives. He then asked Carl, "Where's this ladder you were telling us about?"

"It's here," said Carl. Next to the far wall was a stack of metal rungs. Carl picked up two three foot sections and demonstrated how they fit together by sliding one into the other. A clip was then pushed through holes that kept the ladder together. "The ladder is fifteen feet long once it is put together."

The fellows spent a little time putting together a few sections. "Feels good," said Ray.

"Yes, Captain. I built it myself; it is strong and will get us over the wall."

Just after 1 a.m. Hans came into the front room. "We will be leaving shortly," he announced.

"Good," said Joe. "I'm tired of sitting around."

Everyone else agreed. All day long Ray and the fellows had waited restlessly, hidden in the house playing cards and listening to the radio for the latest war news; by now they were anxious to begin the mission. With nervous, pent up energy they gathered their equipment. A few moments later they were loaded up and ready to move.

"Some of us will have to carry a piece of the ladder," said Axel. George, Jake, Joe, Larry and Carl each took a section, while Ray, Chuck and Axel carried the bags of explosives.

"Good, we are all set," said Hans. Before stepping out the door Hans embraced his sobbing wife and spoke to her in German. Ray didn't need an interpreter to tell him that Hans was reassuring her that everything would be ok.

Once outside Hans looked around and pulled his beanie tight over the top of his head; the town was dark and quiet. "The plant is only about half a mile from here. We will cross through the forest and make our way down to the river's edge."

"Sounds good," said Ray buttoning up his jacket and positioning his "Tommy" gun into a more comfortable position. "Lead on."

Hans led them out of town at a hurried pace across a high, grass covered field that ended at a row of large trees. "It is here that I must leave you. I am going to make my way to the train station and will be waiting for you there. Hans and Axel know the path to the Plant well." Sticking out his hand, Hans and Ray shook. "Good luck, Captain." A quick nod to Axel and Carl and Hans vanished into the darkness.

"Let's go," said Axel taking the lead. In silence they entered the forest following a well-worn path. The thick trees rising high in the night sky blocked out the stars and the moonlight they had been using to light their way.

"How in the hell can you see where you're going?" asked Joe in a whisper.

"Yeah, can't we use a flashlight?" inquired George, nearly tripping over a tree root.

"Carl and I have been down this path many times," replied Axel. "When we were children we would run down it during the summer and swim in the river. Trust me, we know it well."

"Listen, already I can hear the river," said Carl. In silence the group stood, hearing the rushing of water off in the distance.

"Come, we are almost there," said Axel.

A few yards later they came to the edge of the trees and an open field with high grass. Up ahead the river rushed by fast and loud sparkling brilliantly with the reflection of the moon. Off to the left Ray and the fellows got their first look at the Hydro Plant. The compound sat spread out over several acres. The main building was bigger and more imposing in person than it had been in the photographs. A few lights from its second story windows could be seen over the high, daunting walls. A dim light hung over the gated front entrance.

"Come on," said Axel. Crouching low the group sprinted across the open field to an incline that led down to the edge of the river. The roar of rushing water was loud; *Axel was right*, thought Ray as they slid down the incline, *any sounds we might make would definitely be covered by the river*. "This way," said Axel. Now that they were out of the forest the moonlight helped them see a little better. The going was still perilous though. There were large rocks and boulders strewn all about and the footing was unsure. Ray was thankful for the cliff training he and his men had been put through, it helped their balance and kept them from injury.

Through the darkness they made their way over the rocky ground occasionally getting splashed by freezing cold river water. Ray could now clearly see the rear wall and the dam and thousands of gallons of water spilling into the turbine inlets. A few feet before reaching the wall, Axel stopped at a clearing. "This is a good spot to put the ladder together," he said. In just a few seconds they had it pieced together and the retaining clips securely in place. Carrying the ladder in tandem, Axel and Carl placed it against the concrete wall. "You're up, Captain," said Axel. Ray took his queue and climbed the ladder. Carefully he peered over the wall. He could see the rear of the main building. Off to the right a smaller two-story building; the barracks. To the left, against the wall, a high guard tower with the form of an unmoving guard, probably asleep. Ray reached into his pocket and pulled out a heavy pair of wire cutters. With a twang the barbed wire snapped apart and recoiled. Three more strands and the wall was clear. Climbing back down he said, "Joe, you're first. Get your rifle on that guard, if he looks like he spotted us, you kill'em, got it?"

"Yes, Sir," said Joe with a nod. He then climbed the ladder and swung over the wall. Landing on the ground he melted into the darkness. With his back against the brick wall he raised his rifle and put the cross-hairs on the sleeping guard.

"Alright, let's go," said Ray. Quickly he climbed the ladder, heaved himself over and dropped to the ground. In rapid succession, George, Larry, Chuck, Axel and Carl followed. Jake, causing the ladder to bend slightly with his great weight came last. Straddling the wall, he swung the ladder over, handing it down to Axel and Carl before dropping lightly to the ground.

"Our man on the inside has assured me that the door will be unlocked," said Carl.

"Let's hope so," said Ray, "or this is going to be a short night." Ray could see a door to the left of a large sliding metal door that was big enough to drive a truck through.

Giving the area a quick scan, Ray said, "Wait here, I'll check the door." Bent low, he sprinted across the yard coming to a stop at the door. Turning the knob he found that it was unlocked and pulled it open just a crack. Looking in, Ray saw a large, well lit room. Directly in front of him he could see a row of hard-water tanks with hoses and steel tubes protruding from the tops. To the right an open area and a tarp covered transport truck. To the right of the truck were stacks of wooden boxes, many with German writing and red Swastikas emblazoned across the front. Next to the boxes was a large windowed office with four scientists wearing long white lab coats talking with an armed guard.

Clicking the door shut Ray turned and gave a signal. A second later the group was crouched with Ray. "How's it look?" asked Jake.

"Four scientists and a guard in an office."

"A guard?" asked Axel, with a worried look. He then took a quick peek in.

"You're right. We will have to take him down quickly and quietly," said Axel.

"George and Jake, you come with me," said Ray. "We will take the scientists and the guard. Joe, you, Larry and Chuck start laying out the explosives." Ray unslung his pack of C-3 and handed it to Joe. "Axel and Carl, you head downstairs and find those bombs."

"Yes, Captain," replied Axel.

Opening the door, Ray slipped in followed by Jake and George. Staying close to the wall they ran across the building keeping an eye on their enemy. Reaching the other side they crouched behind a row of wooden boxes. From their vantage point they could see the office about fifty feet away and a slightly open door. "I'll take the guard," said Ray, "you two secure the scientists. Remember don't kill them."

"Let's go," urged Ray. In a rush they ran to the door and burst in on the unsuspecting men. Taken by surprise the guard could do nothing but stare point blank at Ray's pistol. Having picked up a smattering of German, Italian and French during his tour in Europe, Ray barked out a harsh command in German, "Sei still!" The guard nodded, indicating he understood that he was to keep silent. Ray quickly stripped the man of his weapons and secured his hands with a length of rope. He then slapped a strip of tape across the guard's mouth and motioned him to sit on the floor. Jake quickly bound the scientists, too, and had them sit next to the guard.

"George, keep an eye on the prisoners."

"Yes, Sir."

"Jake and I are going to help lay the C-3."

Ray found Joe, Chuck and Larry quickly attaching the charges to tanks and laying the connecting wires. With all their previous practice they were fast, efficient and making good time.

"Jake and I will start on the next row," said Ray, tossing a sack of C-3 to Jake. Joe, absorbed in his job said nothing, but gave Ray a nod.

Working fast, Ray and Jake began setting their explosives. In a matter of minutes they had placed and wired half a dozen charges. With the last wire attached, Ray trailed a length of wire over to Joe, who attached it to his wires. With a final twist Joe said, "We're all set. All we have to do is set the time and flick the switch to start the countdown."

Ray wiped sweat from his brow and looked at the tank he was facing. He could see through a sight glass a slow drip of hard-water from a tube that had nearly filled the steel cylinder. Looking down at his watch, he grunted, "Where the hell are Hans and Carl? We gotta go."

Just then the brothers came running up panting hard. "Everything is set, Captain," said Axel. "We have four minutes."

"Good," replied Ray. Squatting down he took hold of the alarm clock. In the quietness he could hear the clock's ticking and the hum of the overhead lights and feel the beating of his heart. With a turn of the dial he set the alarm to go off in three minutes and slid it under the tank. A metallic flick of the lever and the countdown began.

Chapter Eleven
The Hound

"Let's go!" The urgency in Ray's voice was as serious as gunfire. Together the group took off at a run across the building.

"Axel," said Ray as they ran, "you grab the scientists, and meet us at the back door; we'll take them over the wall with us."

"Yes, Captain," replied Axel.

Nearing the office there was suddenly a commotion. "Damn it!" hollered George. Ray spotted the guard darting from the office and heading across the building at a dead run; his hands still tied. A second later came George in pursuit, with a tirade of curses.

"Dempsey!" yelled Ray, "stop him, now." In one smooth motion Joe swung his rifle into position, aimed and fired. The bullet impacted the guard high in the shoulder sending out a spray of crimson. With a shriek he stumbled a few steps, but failed to go down. Before Joe could pull the trigger again the German disappeared behind a row of steel tanks. Joe ran after him. George, still cursing ran by. "What happened," demanded Ray as George sprinted past.

"The bastard knocked me down," snorted George angrily.

Coming around the row of tanks Joe caught sight of the guard and raised his rifle. He didn't like the idea of shooting a man in the back, but had no choice; the guard was headed straight for the red alarm button on the wall. The shot took the guard through the heart. Amazingly he didn't go down. *Damn it*, thought Joe as he aimed for another shot. Stumbling the last few feet the guard hit the wall slamming his shoulder into the alarm button as he fell dying. All at once the building reverberated with a loud ringing.

Ray, Jake, Chuck and Carl stopped at the back door, joined a second later by Axel and four terrified scientists; a moment after that Joe and George came running up. Ray knew they were in a bad situation. It would only take a matter of seconds for the guards to jump out of bed, grab their weapons and surround the building. He thought about making a run out the back door, but knew they would be cut to shreds trying to climb the wall. Opening the door a crack Ray could already see German soldiers half-dressed but armed pouring out of the barracks and heading right toward them. The guard in the tower was frantically shining a bright spotlight all over looking for intruders. Ray closed the door and secured the lock.

"Damn it, there's Germans all over the yard!" screamed Ray.

"We're trapped!" yelled Jake.

Ray eyed his men. Hardened as they were from countless battles, they looked scared. Quickly he scanned the building for an escape route, his eyes stopping on the big transport truck.

"Not quite!" he yelled over the scream of the alarm. "Everyone in the truck, now!" But before they could move, a lethal spray of machinegun fire splattered into the wall next to them; the Germans had opened the front door and were in. Ray, Jake and Larry returned fire as the rest of the fellows took cover behind a stack of boxes.

"Come on!" said Ray leading the way. As a group they made their way behind the cover of boxes until they were directly across from the truck.

"We're gonna have to make a run to the truck," said Ray. "I'll drive, Larry, you ride shotgun. The rest of you jump in the back."

"The moment we take off in that truck we're gonna be cut to pieces," said Joe. "There's at least half a dozen Germans over there."

Ray knew Joe was right. "Alright," said Ray. "Chuck and Larry you watch the back door. The rest of you keep the Germans occupied, Jake and I will clear a path."

Looking at his watch Joe shouted, "We have two minutes and this place is coming down!"

"We'll make it quick," yelled Ray as he and Jake tore off racing across the shop followed by a hail of German lead. Ducking behind a row of tanks Ray sprinted at a reckless pace. He knew that time was short and there was no need for caution; if they didn't get out of here they were dead.

With a turn Ray and Jake came around the last tank -- face to face with half a dozen Germans crouching behind a stack of crates. Even as he was turning, Ray squeezed the trigger of his Thompson. With a burst of muzzle fire one of the Germans went down. Another turned and fired but Ray's momentum carried him past the deadly spray of lead. A split second later, Jake emptied his entire clip of thirty rounds into the five remaining guards. With screams and splatters of blood three fell. Wielding his empty machinegun like a club, Jake sprang on the last two before they could return fire. The butt of his gun crashed into the first soldier's face with a crunching of bone. His return swing caught the second one across the side of the head with a terrible impact that sent him skidding across the floor with his skull crushed in. Without a second to spare Ray wheeled around and sprinted back to the fellows with Jake close behind.

Ray found his men in a furious gunfight with guards that were trying to get in through the back door.

"We can't hold them much longer!" yelled Joe.

"Everyone in the truck now!" hollered Ray. He then sent a continuous burst of bullets at the back door as the fellows ran for the truck. Turning to the scientists, he said, "All of you in the truck, you're coming with us."

One of the scientists replied in English, "Don't worry about us, we will leave out the back door, the guards will not shoot us." He then gave Ray a straight look and said, "Go now, Captain, and good luck."

Ray jumped into the driver's seat, and was relieved to find that the keys were in the ignition. He had thought for a moment that he might have to hot wire it. A quick glance at his watch showed that he only had 30 seconds until the bombs detonated.

With a rumble the engine came to life; a puff of black smoke billowing from its tailpipes. Ray shoved the shifter into first gear and dropped the clutch. The big truck heaved forward. Building up speed Ray slammed the shifter into second gear.

"Hang on!" he yelled at the top of his lungs as he sped toward the sliding metal door. Just then a group of soldiers ran into the building with machineguns blazing. Ray could hear the metallic clang of bullets slamming into the truck. Some of the bullets blew holes through the windshield sending shards of glass raining into the cab. Larry suddenly cried out in pain as he clutched his left shoulder; he was hit. An instant later with the accelerator on the floor and the engine revved up the truck ripped through the door.

Outside, the compound was swarming with German soldiers, who instantly opened fire on the truck. Directly ahead of him Ray could see the front gate. He shifted the truck into third gear; building even more speed. It was then that he saw him a man in a black uniform; a defiant sentry standing before the gate. Ray knew it was Von Richten, "The Hound of the Reich." Raising a machinegun the Hound began firing maniacally. Bright red flames and smoke burst from his gun as bullets tore holes through the truck. Ducking down Ray could just see over the dash. He watched as Richten leaped aside at the last moment and the truck burst through the front gate ripping one of the doors completely off its hinges.

The impact sent the truck sideways and into a slide that lifted the right side wheels off the ground. Only with a tremendous effort was Ray able to turn the wheel and keep the truck from rolling over.

Speeding away Ray turned to Larry; he could see blood soaking through his shirt. "How bad is it?" he asked.

"I think I'm ok, caught me high on the shoulder."

Ray then yelled into the back cargo area, "Is everyone ok?"

"We're alive," yelled Jake, "but Joe was knocked over when we crashed through the gate and hit his head. He's busted up pretty bad and out cold. Chuck is working on him."

Before Ray could say another word a powerful shockwave rocked the big truck followed by the sound of a tremendous boom like the crack of thunder; the bombs had detonated. From his rearview mirror Ray could see a brilliant burst of bright orange flames and smoke lighting up the night sky.

"Axel," yelled Ray as they came to a fork in the road, "which way?"

"Stay to the left, Captain, always to the left. The train station is about four miles."

Ray turned his attention back to driving when suddenly from out of the night came the roar of men on motorcycles racing toward the truck. Ray looked at his rearview mirror and spotted half a dozen bright headlights and like hell hounds on his tail they sped closer.

"It's Von Richten!" yelled Axel, after taking a quick look out the rear of the truck.

Ray hammered down the accelerator and shifted gears, then heard rapid machinegun fire. Everyone in the back flattened themselves behind the heavy steel tailgate as bullets shredded through the canvas covering. Chuck, covering Joe's unconscious body with his, cradled Joe's bleeding head and tried to staunch the flow of blood with a large piece of gauze. "Carl, Axel, George!" yelled Jake over the noise of the motorcycles. "On the count of three we're gonna blast these sons-of-bitches."

Crawling up next to Jake, Carl and Axel readied their weapons. Jake gave George a nod. "One, two, three!" he yelled. All four men jumped up. At the same time Jake and Carl pushed aside the canvas flaps. Following a few yards behind were four Germans on bikes. Two were armed with pistols, the third a submachine gun. The one in the lead was holding a German stick grenade and trying desperately to throttle his bike close enough to throw it in.

In a blaze of hell fire, bullets, blood and screams everyone fired and a grenade was thrown. Two of the motorcycle riders went down instantly riddled with machinegun bullets. The third rider sprayed a dozen bullets, several of them striking Carl in the middle of his chest. "Carl!" yelled Axel as both brothers fell back. With a curse George returned fire hitting the German half a dozen times across the chest and neck, sending him and his bike tumbling into the dirt.

The fourth rider gunned the throttle hard pulling within a few feet of the speeding truck. Raising the grenade to his mouth he yanked the pull-cord with his teeth and threw. Seeing what was happening Jake swung his Thompson toward the German and squeezed the trigger, but was out of bullets. Dropping his machinegun he quick-drew his pistol and fired twice, the bullets striking the German's head just as the grenade flew past landing in the truck.

Both Jake and George wheeled around knowing they only had a few seconds to grab the grenade and toss it out, but in the dark of the truck in was nearly impossible to see. Suddenly, after hitting a jolting bump in the road the grenade rolled into view right next to Chuck and Joe. "Right here!" shouted Chuck as he covered Joe's body, tensing for the inevitable explosion. Spotting the grenade first, George knew he would never be able to grab it quickly enough and toss it out. Leaping across the bed of the truck he kicked it with his left leg, sending it back under the wooden seats. A fraction of a second later it detonated with a loud crack and a flash of bright light, the seats and George's leg taking the brunt of the explosion. The force of the grenade blew George across the truck where he landed in a heap next to Axel and Carl; his act had saved Joe and Chuck.

"George!" screamed Jake. Turning George over, Jake could see that his leg was a gory mess of shrapnel, and shredded red flesh. Gritting his teeth George's face was etched with intense pain and agony, but tough as nails he didn't make a sound.

"Chuck!" yelled Jake. "George needs your help." Dragging his medical pack over Chuck began pulling out rolls of bandages.

Through the insanity of machineguns, screams and explosions Ray failed to notice the motorcycle that raced up next to him, until it was too late. It was the loud bang of gunfire and the searing pain of a bullet in his hip that drew his attention away from driving. Looking over he spotted Von Richten, Luger in hand and hell fire in his eyes, aiming for another shot. Drawing his .45 Ray steered with one hand and fired with the other. Richten let off the throttle and fell back disappearing into the night; Ray's bullets hit empty air. To the right another motorcycle sped up next to Larry's door, its rider firing recklessly while Larry ducked down.

Spotting the rider Ray turned the steering wheel hard sending the truck crashing into the bike. With a scream both man and bike ricochet head on into a tree with a loud crash. And then everything was quiet. The only sound was the roar of the truck's engine. Just then Ray came to another fork in the road and yanked the wheel to the left.

"Where's the Hound?" yelled Ray looking around frantically.

"I don't see him," said Larry. "Maybe he went down."

Ray thought for a moment, but with all the excitement he wasn't sure.

Ignoring their wounds Ray and Larry held their guns ready, wary for another round of attacks. Looking down Ray could see blood soaking through his pants.

"Jake! What's going on back there?"

"You better step on it, Ray," came Jake's booming voice. "Joe, Carl and George are in bad shape."

Nearly in a panic Ray stepped on the accelerator forcing the big truck to go faster. Down the long dark road he raced at breakneck speeds; the only thought on his mind was saving his friends. Rounding a large group of trees he spotted a long train and a station up ahead.

"There it is," said Larry pointing.

Just a few yards from the train Ray slammed on the brakes and put the truck into a slide that kicked up a shower of dirt. Coming to a stop he and Larry sat for a moment scanning the area; the station was dark, and quiet.

"Let's go," said Ray. With great difficulty he opened his door and swung himself out of the truck. The moment he put weight on his leg he toppled over, in excruciating pain.

"On your feet," said Larry, "I got you." With one arm over Larry's shoulder Ray got to his feet, together they made their way to the back of the truck. Jake was already out and in the process of unloading George. Ray could see that George was in massive pain as Jake lowered him to the ground. But with his jaw clenched tightly he refused to mutter even a sound. Jake then helped Chuck unload the bloodied and still dazed Joe.

"Come on, Axel," said Jake. Yanking the canvas flap aside Jake could see Axel and Carl in the back of the truck. Neither was moving. With a leap Jake jumped into the back. "Axel," he called. Still no response. Pulling Axel off his brother it was then that Jake could see that Axel had been shot through the chest at some point. Both brothers were dead.

"They're both dead," said Jake as he jumped from the truck. For a second nobody said a word.

"Damn it," said Ray. "There's nothing we can do for them now. We gotta go."

"He's right," said Chuck urgently. "We need to leave now, we need a hospital."

"Let's get to the train," said Ray. "Jake, you grab George."

"Yes, Sir," replied Jake.

"Chuck, you get Joe loaded."

"Yes, sir," replied Chuck.

Ray looked around up and down the tracks and at his watch. "Where the hell is Hans?" he said with frustration in his voice. "He was supposed to be here before us."

Suddenly a deep, sinister German voice broke the night's silence. "He is here, Captain." From behind a freight car two men stepped out of the darkness; Hans first with a look of terror in his eyes, and the Hound right behind him with his Luger against the back of Hans's head.

"Hans!" exclaimed Ray.

"Drop your weapons now!" screamed the Hound.

Both Ray and Jake hesitated as they went for their guns.

"Don't do it, Captain, shoot him now," pleaded Hans.

"Silence!" yelled Von Richten. Suddenly he pointed his gun at Jake and fired.

As if time had slowed, Ray saw the shot pierce Jake's chest sending him staggering back a few steps. With a grunt he fell to his knees.

"Jake!" The words were torn from Ray's mouth. Letting go of Larry he fell to the ground.

"As I said before, drop your weapons, now! Or I will shoot another."

Beaten, they did as they were told.

"Very well," said Von Richten with a smile. He then shoved Hans forward causing him to fall near Ray. "You sit in the dirt with the rest of the dogs."

Standing before them he said, "I figured you would try to escape using the train. It is the only way out of Germany. So I took a…how do you say, a short-cut to beat you here. I found this one hiding and had just enough time to question him before you arrived."

Stepping closer the Hound asked, "Now, which one of you is Captain Miller?"

Ray looked up at Richten and replied in a voice filled with loathing, "I am."

Richten turned his eyes on Ray and spoke. "Captain, let me be the first to congratulate you and your men on a successful mission. It appears that you have destroyed my entire supply of hard-water. You may think that you have won a great victory, but we Germans are resilient, we will rebuild, we will produce more hard-water. And America will burn."

"Go to hell," said Ray.

"I intend to, Captain. For my failure to safeguard the hydro-plant I will no doubt be executed. The Fuhrer does not take failure lightly. My one consolation, however, will be knowing that you and your men will be there before me." He then aimed his gun at Ray.

It was then that Jake struck as suddenly as the flash of a thunderbolt. One moment he was still, the next he was a blur of action. Two tigerish strides brought him within striking distance of the Hound. His left hand shot out grabbing hold of Richten's right wrist forcing it up just as the gun fired. His right hand locked on the Hound's throat with an iron grip.

Instantly the two were a frenzy of action. Richten tried frantically to tear his hand free and bring his gun into play as Jake forced him back violently towards the train. Unable to free his hand the Hound brought his knee up hard into Jake's stomach and then into his groin. The excruciating pain was enough to weaken Jake for just a moment; long enough for the Hound to yank his hand free. Swinging the gun up, Richten's eyes blazed with an evil light and his lips pulled back into an animal like snarl. Savagely he brought the handle of the pistol crashing down onto the side of Jake's head. Blood splattered and the big man stumbled, but he maintained his grip on Richten's throat. Again the Hound brutally hammered the gun into the side of Jake's head. Only Jake's incredible vitality kept him up, any other man would have fallen.

For an instant the battle was poised, its outcome uncertain. And then through a thick fog of pain and confusion Jake heard Ray scream his name. The sound of his friend's voice brought his addled senses rushing back just in time to see the Hound swinging his pistol down for a final crushing blow. But before it could land Jake grabbed hold of the Hound's wrist, stopping the swing in mid-air.

With a powerful surge of strength he bent the wrist back until the bone snapped. Von Richten cried out in pain, his gun dropping from nerveless fingers. Releasing the wrist Jake's hand clamped on the Hound's throat and he exerted his gigantic strength.

Like a drowning man Richten fought desperately for his life. He tried to pry away those inexorable fingers that were crushing the life out of him, but his efforts were in vain. Deeper and deeper those terrible fingers ground like a hangman's noose into his yielding neck muscles. A look of panic and fear came to the Hound's eyes, they were growing distended and his face was turning blue.

Using the last of his waning strength Jake lifted the Hound off his feet and drove him back until he slammed into the steel train coupling. Overcome with an unreasoning fury that only a man who fights for his very life could comprehend, Jake let out an inhuman scream. He then forced the Hound's head back until his grisly face stared up into the night sky and his neck snapped like a rotten branch.

Breathing heavily, Jake dropped Richten's flopping corpse to the ground. Turning, he staggered back towards the fellows. For a moment his face had the look of pure, untamed savagery and then a semblance of sanity returned to his eyes just before he collapsed.

Chuck and Hans ran to him. Ray, unable to stand, crawled his way to Jake's side. "Hans! Larry!" said Chuck. "Grab hold of him quickly; let's get him on the train." With a great heave the three of them lifted Jake's huge body onto the freight car. George, half delirious and in shock was next, then Joe and finally Ray.

"I'll get the train going," said Hans as he took off at a run.

Once on the train Ray dragged himself to Jake's side. Lifting the big man's head he placed it on his lap. He saw a lot of blood and could tell that Jake's breathing was labored and shallow. Chuck ripped open Jake's blood-soaked shirt and examined the wound.

"How bad is it?" asked Ray.

Chuck gave Ray a distressed look and shook his head. "There's nothing I can do. I don't know how he made it this far, the shot should have killed him instantly."

Suddenly Jake opened his eyes and focused on Ray's face. In a voice hardly above a whisper he asked, "Did everyone make it?"

"Yeah, Jake, everyone made it, everyone is safe because of you."

"Good," he said with his familiar crocked smile.

"I just want to go home now, Ray."

"We are, Jake, we're going home. You just hang on, ok?"

"Ok, Ray."

And with that Ray felt Jake's enormous body tremble and go slack and he knew that Jake was gone. Ray sat for a moment embracing his friend, rocking him back and forth, tears running down his dirt stained face. With a jolt and a squeaking of wheels the train began to move.

Lost in the epic tale it took a moment for Cody to realize that his grandfather had stopped talking. Ray sat slumped in his chair. To Cody his grandfather looked like a beaten fighter that had gone fifteen grueling rounds, only to hear that he had lost the fight. The boy was then shocked to see that his grandfather was crying quietly.

Astonished by the outpouring of emotions from such a tough man, Cody was at a loss for a moment as to how to react. And then it came to him. Without a word he knelt down in front of his grandfather and embraced him. He could feel his body tremble as the emotions that had been locked away like a terrible secret spilled out and his tormented soul was exposed for the first time in fifty-years. Cody could feel grief, shame, and regret as they shared the moment. Quietly the boy whispered, "Grandpa, it wasn't your fault."

"I promised him I would get him back home," Ray said between sobs.

"It wasn't your fault. You did everything you could, Grandpa."

"I never got a chance to thank him for getting us out of there."

"It's ok, Grandpa, Jake knows."

For a moment longer Ray hugged his grandson and then let go. In the dim light of the front room Cody could see that he looked older, strained, and weary.

"Are you all right?" asked the boy.

"I'm ok," Ray replied in a voice overwrought with emotions. Using the back of his hand he wiped away the warm tears that had ran down his cheek. "Just give me a second."

"Are you sure you want to keep going?" asked Cody.

"Yeah, I'm sure," answered Ray.

Cody sat back on the couch. His grandfather took a deep breath and continued with his story.

Ray awoke to a dull throbbing pain from his hip. He was in a bed with clean white sheets and a thick warm blanket; *a hospital* he thought. To his right was George. To his left was Joe with a large white bandage on his head. And one bed over was Larry; they were all sleeping. Chuck sat next to his bed looking through a newspaper even though it was in Polish. "Chuck," said Ray, his voice hoarse and dry. "What happened? Where are we?"

Ray had a clear memory of everything that had happened up to the point of the train leaving Germany; after that, only fragmented bits and pieces of memory. Chuck lowered his paper. "Glad to see you're awake, Sir. We're in a hospital, in Poland; you've been asleep for two days."

"Two days?" asked Ray a little surprised.

"Yes, Sir, after we arrived in Poland they rushed everyone to the hospital, good thing too, Joe and George were nearly dead with blood loss. They operated on you to remove the bullet that was lodged in your hip. The good news is you should make a full recovery."

"What about the fellows?"

Chuck looked downcast for a moment and leaned in close to Ray. When he spoke his voice was barely more than a whisper. "They had to take George's leg; it was too damaged by the German grenade to be saved. As you can imagine, he wasn't too happy. They operated on Larry, too, took a bullet from his shoulder. The doctor says he may never have full use of his arm, but he'll live. Joe's suffering from a severe concussion, doesn't remember most of what happened. It took seventy-five stitches to close his wound."

Ray sat quiet for a moment. "What did they do with Jake?" he asked.

"Ray," said Chuck, "you don't have to deal with this right now, you need rest."

"What did they do with him, Chuck?" Ray's voice was rising a little.

"They're sending him home to be buried in the old cemetery outside of town, by the red church, you know the one." Ray nodded and turned to his side. Chuck knew that the conversation was over.

The next day Ray was up eating lunch along with the fellows and listening to George gripe about losing his leg, when much to everyone's surprise in walked General Barrack and Basil Edmonds followed by the head doctor, several bodyguards and Hans.

"Afternoon, men," said Barrack in his booming voice. "Glad to see you're up and looking well."

"Gentlemen," said Basil.

"Basil and I wanted to come here personally to thank and congratulate you men on a successful mission. We received word that the Hydro-plant's entire store of hard-water was completely wiped out. We also learned that the two bombs were also destroyed. Because of you men the Germans' Atomic project has been dealt a crippling blow and Hitler's dreams of world conquest are coming to an end." Barrack then paused and gave them a piercing look filled with pride and said, "You saved the world. You men are heroes."

Barrack then paused and turned his attention to Ray. "I can't tell you how sorry I am to hear about Jake. From what Hans told Basil and I it was because of Jake that you men were able to escape from the Hound. I've spoken with President Roosevelt. He has decided to award Jake the Congressional Medal of Honor."

"He deserves it," was Ray's only response.

"The rest of you men will be awarded the Distinguished Service Cross, along with other medals, at a ceremony held at the White House a week from now."

"The White House?" asked Chuck. "You mean we're going home?"

"That's right," said Barrack. "For you men the war is over."

"What about Carl and Axel?" asked Ray. "They gave their lives for the mission."

"They will be honored as well," replied Basil.

"And believe me, Captain," said Hans. "Their sacrifice will not be forgotten. When this war is over they will go down in German history as heroes."

Ray sat back in his recliner, lost in reflective thought not saying a word. Cody knew that the story was over. With a deep breath his grandfather got up from his recliner and said, "It's been quite a day, I think I'm ready for bed."

"Yeah," agreed the boy. "I think you're right."

Standing up they hugged once more and walked off to their rooms. Looking back before his grandfather closed his door, Cody asked, "Are you sure you're going to be ok, Grandpa?"

"I am now," answered Ray. And for the first time ever, Cody saw his grandfather smile.

Coming into the front room the next morning Cody found it empty but he could hear his grandfather in his bedroom getting dressed. Turning the TV on he sat for a while watching the weatherman give his prediction for a warm, sunny day. As he sat he thought about the last few days spent with his grandfather. The visit had turned out to be something that he could have never imagined. And he realized that he was sad knowing that his father would be picking him up in just a matter of hours.

A few minutes later Cody was blown away when his grandfather stepped into the front room wearing a full dress Army uniform. Deep green, wrinkle free and creased precisely it had been perfectly preserved for fifty-years. Like some noble king out of legend he stood. For a moment the boy was too awed to speak. Finally he stood up. "Wow! You look great." His gaze then dropped to the cluster of medals that sparkled across his grandfather's chest. Three were in the shape of stars; two were bright silver and one a dark bronze. Another of brilliant gold was in the shape of a cross with an eagle in the center, proudly spreading its wings. Below the mighty bird was engraved the words, "For Valor." Next to it were two purple ones in the shape of hearts with the gold image of a man's head in the center. Pinned below them was a glimmering golden star encircled with a green laurel wreath, with tiny white stars clustered in its center. And next to it was a majestic golden eagle surrounded by a shining band of blue with gold words that read: "For Distinguished Service."

As if he were touching something fragile, Cody brushed his finger across one of the medals and thought, *the great halls of Valhalla must shine with the same kind of light.*

"Grandpa, how did you get all of these medals?" he asked, in a voice full of wonder and amazement.

"Well, I got most of them for bravery, or maybe for being stupid," he said with a chuckle.

"And I got a couple of them for being shot up a few times."

Rubbing his mid-section Ray commented, "It's a little tighter than I remember; guess I put on a few pounds in the last fifty-years."

Still staring in admiration, Cody said, "Are you kidding me, you look awesome."

"Well, I appreciate that. You ready to go?"

"I sure am," said Cody excitedly.

Assuming that they were headed for the donut shop Cody was surprised when they drove right past it.

"Where we headed, Grandpa?" he asked curiously all the while looking back longingly at the passing donut shop; his dreams of hot chocolate and a sweet cinnamon roll fading in the distance.

"A place I should have gone to a long time ago," he answered in a solemn tone.

It only took them a few miles to leave the small town behind. They traveled in silence down an old pothole riddled two-lane blacktop road. At an intersection Ray turned right and continued driving for several more miles. Gradually a building came into view. As they neared, Cody could see that it was a small red church with white window frames and a high sloping roof. It was resting comfortably next to a group of massive oak trees. Parked next to the building were two pickup trucks. Cody recognized one of them as Joe's. Pulling alongside the boy could see Chuck and Joe seated in Joe's truck. Without a word Ray and Cody got out. Joe and Chuck got out as well and much to Cody's surprise they too were dressed in Army uniforms. And like his grandfather they glittered with medals.

"Morning, Cody," said Joe and Chuck simultaneously.

"Hi," replied the boy.

"Where's George?" asked Ray.

"He's coming," said Joe.

"You know him, Sir he's always late," added Chuck.

For a minute the four stood in silence and then their attention was drawn to an approaching car.

"There he is," said Joe.

George pulled up in his old white Cadillac. Fumbling with his crutches he got out of his car with a string of well-chosen curse words. Like the others he was in a full dress uniform and had an impressive display of awards.

"Morning, Sir," he said to Ray as he made his way to the group. He then gave Joe and Chuck a nod and said to Cody, "Morning, kid."

"Hi," replied Cody.

George then adjusted his shirt and tucked it in a little better saying, "Damn uniform must have shrunk. I don't remember it being this tight."

"Shrunk," said Chuck, "it didn't shrink; you just got fatter, too many of those donuts."

"Listen here, Chuck, you just go to hell," replied George.

Suppressing a smile, Ray cut-in saying, "Are we ready?"

George and Chuck fell silent

"The question, Sir," asked Joe "is, are you?"

Ray took a deep breath and thought for a moment before he answered, "I believe I am."

"Then lead the way, Sir," said Joe.

Cody followed behind as they walked past the church and out into a graveyard with hundreds of different shaped headstones. Following a well-worn path they eventually came to a stop in front of a large grey stone that was inscribed: Jake W. Cutter 1917-1944. Below the name it read: U.S. Army, Congressional Medal of Honor. Nobody spoke a word; they just stood in peaceful silence. And then suddenly the wind picked up and the leaves on the trees swayed rhythmically; a moment later Cody could feel a presence. It was the same feeling he had experienced when he held Jake's Medal, except this time he was filled with a feeling of happiness.

Looking at the fellows he knew that all of them could feel the same sensation. His grandfather looked at all of them with a smile. Cody could see that the sadness that his grandfather had carried in his eyes was gone and he knew that it would never return. Joe noticed it to. Looking over at Cody their eyes met and he gave the boy a sly wink. Several peaceful moments passed and Ray suddenly knelt down and kissed the headstone. Quietly he whispered, "Thank you." From his pocket he then pulled out a framed black and white picture that had all five of them in it and set it against the headstone. As Ray stood back up Cody looked at him and said, "Grandpa, you did keep your promise; you brought everyone back home."

Ray smiled at his grandson. "I think we're done here."

Back at their cars, Ray said, "See you fellows at the donut shop."

"Ok," said Joe. "I'm sure we're gonna to cause quite a commotion," he said with a laugh.

"Yeah, wait till they get a load of us," added George.

Pulling up to the donut shop Cody looked at his grandfather and said, "You ready, Grandpa?"

"You bet I am," he replied with a smile.

Getting out of the truck they were joined by Joe, George and Chuck. Walking in, Doris and all the regulars gave them wide-eyed stares as they made their way to their customary bench and sat down. Hurrying over to their table Doris said, "I can't believe what I'm seeing. I haven't seen you boys dressed in your uniforms since you came back from the war. What's the occasion?"

Ray looked at the fellows he said, "We just felt that it was time to pay our respects to a fallen comrade and finally tell our story."

A short time later they were surrounded by a large group of curious customers who had little or no idea that these four men had fought in World War II. Like celebrities they sat sipping coffee, eating donuts and answering dozens of questions about the war and their numerous medals. To the enthralled group they told the heroic story of Operation Nighthawk. About how they destroyed the hydro-plant and how big Jake, the famous football player, had saved them all. And finally the mystery of how George had really lost his leg was revealed.

A couple of hours later Cody stood in front of the donut shop and said goodbye to Joe, George and Chuck. It was with a heavy heart that he shook each of their hands.

"You make sure you come back and see us next time you're in town," said Joe. "We'll be right here at the donut shop."

"I will," said Cody. "I promise."

"Yeah, and you still need to out-fish me," said George.

"Out-fish you?" said Chuck with a chuckle. "That should be easy, Stubby"

"Listen here Charles, you just keep your mouth shut," retorted George. For a moment they all laughed.

Back at home Ray changed into his civilian clothes. Walking into the front room he found Cody looking through his movies.

"You want to watch one?" asked Ray. "We have a few hours before your dad gets here."

"Sure," said Cody. "How about this one? The Magnificent Seven. Looks pretty good."

"It is," said Ray, "and it's one of my favorites."

After the movie Cody gathered his things and set them on the couch.

"Well, I hope your visit wasn't too awful," said Ray as they sat and waited for Mike.

"It wasn't, actually it was great!" said Cody.

A second later a loud knock came from the front door. "Must be your dad," said Ray.

"Come on in!" shouted Ray.

A second later Mike entered. "Hi," he said.

"Hey, Dad," said Cody getting up and giving him a hug.

"Dad, how you doing?" asked Mike as he sat down.

"Great," said Ray with a broad smile. For a second Mike thought it was strange that his dad was smiling but he quickly dismissed it.

"How was Cody? Did he give you a hard time?"

"Oh, just a little." Ray and Cody then shared a quick glance.

For a while they sat visiting and talking about what they did for the last week, especially about the big fish Cody caught and how he fixed Mike's old ten-speed bicycle, but neither Cody nor his grandfather made mention of any top secret missions.

After some time Mike said, "Well, we better get going, we have a long drive and I have work tomorrow."

"Alright," said Ray as they made their way outside to Mike's car.

Before getting into his car Mike gave his dad a hug and much to his astonishment Ray returned the hug warmly and whispered, "I love you, son."

Mike, thinking something was wrong, gave his dad a quizzical look and asked, "You feeling ok, Dad?"

"I'm fine, son," he answered with a grin.

"Ok," replied Mike with a skeptical look as he got into his car.

Cody stood before his grandfather and embraced him. "I'm getting my license in a couple of weeks; maybe I can drive up here and spend a few more days with you, before the summer is over."

"I would like that," said Ray.

"Alright, I guess I'll see you then."

As he turned to leave his grandfather stopped him, saying, "Before you go I want to say something."

"Yeah, what is it, Grandpa?"

"I want to thank you."

"For what?" the boy asked questioningly.

"For saving me," replied his grandfather.

Cody thought for a moment and replied, "You're welcome, Grandpa."

"And one other thing, I want to give this to you." From his pocket Ray pulled out the wooden box that contained Jake's Medal of Honor and handed it to his grandson.

"Grandpa, I, I can't accept this. It's not mine and I didn't do anything to deserve it."

Looking his grandson in the eyes, Ray said, "Yes you did, you stood up to me, you showed courage and valor. You take it and you keep it. I'll tell you one more thing, Jake would have liked you and he would be proud to know that you have that."

"He does know, Grandpa."

"I believe you're right," said Ray.

After a quick hug Cody jumped into the car; with a wave they were off.

"What was that all about," asked Mike. "Is Grandpa feeling ok? He was acting a little strange. And what did he give you?"

"Oh, just a medal," said the boy.

"A medal? What kind of medal?"

"A Medal of Honor."

"A Medal of Honor? A real Medal of Honor? Who's Medal of Honor?"

With a big smile on his face Cody turned to his dad and said, "Dad, if you want to know you're going to have to ask Grandpa."

www.ingramcontent.com/pod-product-compliance
Lightning Source LLC
Chambersburg PA
CBHW070623120726
47909CB00004B/1300